Dickie Bird MBE

FROM THE PAVILION END

WEIDENFELD AND NICOLSON
LONDON

Contents

Foreword
by Brian Johnston

I can think of few people – if any – better qualified than Dickie Bird to write a book on cricket humour. He is famous throughout the cricket world for. his fair and unbiased umpiring. He is arguably the best in the world and certainly the most respected and best loved. He knows what it's all about out in the middle, after displaying his skills as a batsman first with his native Yorkshire and then with Leicestershire. He is probably the only batsman ever to be dropped from a side after making 181 not out. This happened to him in 1959 when he took Ken Taylor's place in the Yorkshire side, as Ken was away playing for MCC. Dickie made his 181 not out against Glamorgan at Bradford, and *Wisden* called him a 'promising colt'. Ken was back in the next match and Dickie was dropped.

But it's not his achievements that make Dickie so qualified to write this book. It's his character. He is a very funny man. He is a bundle of energy, highly strung, is never still and always hopping about like an agitated sparrow. His eyes dart here and there and he hardly ever stops talking. Much of his conversation is in the form of questions: 'What shall I do? What about so and so? What do you think?' He is the world's worst worrier and I always look forward to a Test match in which he is umpiring.

As soon as I arrive at the ground I make a bee-line for the umpires' room to say good morning to Dickie and his two colleagues. (They have a reserve umpire at Tests these days.) Dickie will have been there for several hours. He is very much an early Bird. When umpiring his first Test at the Oval he arrived there at 5.30 a.m. and not surprisingly the club's gates were locked. He tried to climb over them and was promptly arrested by a policeman.

Anyhow in the umpires' room Dickie will be 'relaxing' in a chair but with his hands never still. He'll either be twiddling his hair with his fingers, or scratching his nose. He is thinking of the long day ahead and dreading that he may have to call the players off for bad light. So I can never resist telling him that the latest weather forecasts say that heavy clouds and rain are on their way from the south-west. This immediately starts him off with 'What shall I do, Johnners? Do you really think there will be bad light?' I probably say, 'Yes Dickie. I wouldn't be in your shoes today. I wouldn't fancy facing the boos from this large crowd.'

But of course this is only Dickie acting – once out in the middle he becomes the great Test umpire that he is. But he can't hide his personality, and he is a commentator's joy. There's his famous white cap. He keeps plenty of spares, as they are a collector's item and regularly get pinched. A big West Indian spectator once snatched the cap from Dickie's head during one of those mad dashes to the pavilion at the end of a one-day Final at Lord's. The next day Dickie saw this large West Indian in a bus wearing the cap, but wisely decided not to say anything – for once!

He is always chatting away to someone in the field and as he stands at the bowler's end he thrusts his arms out in front of him, rather as if shooting his cuffs. If there is a run he gets quickly into the right position to give a decision. He runs with a stiff back, with tiny steps and arms pumping at his side. He usually runs backwards at tremendous speed, and would undoubtedly win a gold medal if there was a backward 100 metres in the Olympic Games.

One of his greatest moments was during the bomb scare during the second Test at Lord's vs. West Indies in 1976. Everyone was asked to leave the ground whilst the police searched the stands. Out in the middle the covers had been put on the pitch and the whole playing area was empty except for a small figure perched on top of the covers. It was Dickie, refusing to be put off by a mere bomb threat, and determined to show the world that you can't tell an umpire what to do.

He lives in his spotlessly clean and neat house in his beloved Barnsley where everyone knows him, and he knows everyone. But he does have one problem. When he bought the house the previous owners took with them their pair of peacocks. But alas it wasn't long before they flew back to their own home, and Dickie has been saddled with them ever since. They awake him and his neighbours with their loud squawks at five o'clock every morning. They eat the grapes and fruit in his neighbours' gardens, and to top it all last year, started to breed. Whether Dickie takes it in turns to sit on the two eggs I'm not sure. But he does give a superb impression of their squawks. He was once giving a demonstration in the umpires' room at the Oval, so I recorded it, and during a lull in play, played it to the astonished listeners. They never thought they would hear a Test umpire squawking like a peacock. He gets in a terrible state about them. 'What shall I do, Johnners? They're driving me mad. I can't get any sleep.'

Dickie is a lovable man and always a joy to meet. But remember behind all the fun and laughter is one of the world's best cricket umpires – who is never brow-beaten by loud threatening appeals and only gives a man out if he is *absolutely sure*. He can too be very strict with bowlers who run down the pitch or bowl too many bouncers. He stands no nonsense from anyone.

I am absolutely sure you will enjoy this book. But I have one regret. Instead of you reading the stories, I only wish you could hear Dickie himself telling them in his own inimitable way, in his delightful Yorkshire accent.

Brian Johnston

Acknowledgements

There are many people who have helped me in the production of this book with their advice and encouragement, and my thanks go to all of them. I would particularly like to thank John Callaghan, sports correspondent of the *Yorkshire Evening Post*, with whom I collaborated closely throughout. My thanks also to Larry for providing the illustrations; Roy Ullyett of the *Daily Express* for permission to use the cartoon on the title page; Brian Johnston for kindly contributing the foreword; and Alan Smith, chief executive of the Test and County Cricket Board.

Introduction

I wonder who first said 'Cricket's a funny game.' Probably he was directly related to all the other people who said the same concerning soccer, golf, rugby and most other sports. There is, though, something special about cricket, and I don't think I am being particularly biased.

It is without doubt more at the mercy of the weather, for one downpour of half an hour can wash out a whole day's play. This is very serious whether you are a spectator who has paid a lot of money and travelled a long way to see a big match, or just a club player who has waited all week for your big chance out in the middle. You need a sense of humour to survive.

Then there is the question of the umpire's decision, especially if you happen to be a batsman. I can't think of another sport in which an individual can be put virtually out of the action by the judgment of one man. A soccer referee might well award a penalty which leads to the only goal of a game, but unless he commits a very bad foul or suffers some injury, every player knows he will be on the field for ninety minutes, actively involved.

I have always argued that umpires, both at Test level and on the village green, are by and large very fair and honest men, but they do make mistakes. If you take things too much to heart, therefore, cricket is not for you. It is a game to be enjoyed to the full in the best possible spirit, which means having a laugh and a joke after the keenest competition.

I understand that Brian Rix, the very funny actor, played in a charity match at Hull, his native town. Brian will certainly correct me if I am wrong, but as I heard it the intention of the opposition was to give him at least one off the mark because a lot of spectators had turned up to see him bat. The bowler duly received his instructions and offered a gentle long hop when Brian took his turn at the wicket. Unfortunately, Brian, perhaps a bit anxious, played all round the ball and was well bowled. 'Blimey,' said the unrepentant offender. 'You didn't say he couldn't bat at all. It would have needed a miracle to give him a few runs.'

The thing about stories of that sort is that they expand as they do the rounds, but I know for a fact that Brian is very keen on cricket and I am sure that he will have enlivened many an afternoon. In fact, cricket is extremely popular with actors and entertainers, who have their own societies and teams which raise money for charity in addition to giving a lot of pleasure.

More often than not, however, it's a very serious business out in the middle, no matter how humble the performers, and no professional ever likes to lose.

Some little time ago, the Yorkshire committee met the Press at Headingley in a friendly fixture which came about as the result of a light-hearted challenge. The county club have a large committee and also a substantial band of travelling reporters, so there was no difficulty in selecting two elevens. Inevitably, Brian Close, as chairman of the cricket sub-committee, captained his team which took in a wide range of talent.

Brian, giving no quarter, scored fifty in a useful committee total and the Press struggled when their turn came to bat. Eventually, with one over remaining they were 37 runs adrift, a point Closey checked carefully with the scorers. He then offered the ball to the county president Viscount Mountgarret, who had earlier been run out in somewhat unfortunate circumstances by the former England captain.

The president's first ball was called as a wide and, no doubt because he was a shade out of practice, his second was a friendly leg-stump half volley which David Warner, the cricket correspondent of the Bradford *Telegraph and Argus,* struck high into the rows of empty seats on the Western Terrace for six. Sensing that, although still very remote, the possibility of a tie had now arisen, Brian marched resolutely up to the president and instructed: 'For heaven's sake, pull yourself together and get it outside the offstump.' Viscount Mountgarret successfully did just that, but the Press team were left to wonder just what Closey would have done had the president been struck for another six.

That sort of fixture contains much of the magic of cricket for me – those taking part playing because they love it, with nothing at stake but a bit of pride. There must have been thousands of similar games down the years and Arthur Mitchell, the Yorkshire and England batsman who became county coach, attended one. He watched with interest as mid-on kept allowing the ball to go past him before turning to chase it. 'I'll give you a bit of advice,' he said to the fielding captain during the tea interval 'Never put a piano player in front of the bat, they won't get their hands hurt.'

I suppose sport in general rouses the passions more than most things in life, but cricket, in my experience, has a particular hold over those who fall under its spell. Possibly because the season is comparatively short and because every precious moment has to be snatched, enthusiasts devote all their spare moments – and some not exactly spare at all – to playing or organising or administrating.

A certain Mr Michael Rowley, of Wolverhampton, must have been such a man, for I recall reading about him in the newspapers a good number of years ago. His wife obtained a divorce on the grounds that he had become obsessed with the game. 'I had just had enough of it,' she said in court, but her husband did not appear. He was in Torquay turning out with the Worcestershire Marauders! When asked to comment, he merely said: 'I cannot stop, we have got to get on with the game.'

Thousands of wives accept the role as cricket widows between April and September, although a lot make the best of a bad job and join in the social side of things, often becoming tea ladies. They, of course, are very important in the overall scheme of things. The car park at New Road, Worcester, has a few spaces reserved for them, a state of affairs challenged by an anxious reporter trying to get his car into the ground for an important fixture. 'Sorry, sir, you can't come in, there's no space left,' said the attendant. 'Surely you don't need all this room for tea ladies,' suggested the journalist. 'Oh yes we do,' came the reply. 'I'll tell you, it's a lot more important that we get our tea than you get anything in the paper.'

That, without doubt, was a case of a man getting his priorities right, and in Yorkshire we have never had any difficulties in that direction. Cricket comes first and always has done if local history is to be relied upon. It is, however, significant that one of the earliest references to the game being played within the county – 1751 – records the fact that: 'The Sheffield authorities engaged professional cricketers to amuse the populace and so draw them away from cock-fighting exhibitions.'

That interesting information comes from a newspaper cutting and underlines that from the beginning those who showed any ability expected to be rewarded for their efforts. There has never been much point in 'laikin' for nowt'. In fact, nothing is for nothing, as Roy Genders discovered when he began to write his book, *League Cricket in England,* in 1952.

Roy had been an occasional county player with Derbyshire, Worcestershire and Somerset, but it was more as a league batsman that he earned recognition. As he researched his subject he found that obtaining any assistance from Yorkshire was like getting blood from a stone. He wrote to the Huddersfield League only to receive the following reply from their secretary: 'I regret I am not prepared to spend my valuable time working for a stranger. If you will forward 1s. 6d. [seven and a half pence today] for *Sixty Years of Huddersfield Cricket,* just published, plus 6d for the league handbook, plus 4d. postage, then I will forward the same to you.' Well, at least Roy knew where he stood.

The annual Roses contests between Yorkshire and Lancashire have been of paramount importance, overshadowing even the rivalry between England and Australia so far as all those within the two counties are concerned. Legend has it that the players said 'Good morning' on the first day, 'Goodbye' on the last and confined themselves to 'How's that?' in between. Relations may be a bit more cordial in the 1980s, but neither side likes to lose.

Emmott Robinson, arguably the greatest of all Yorkshire characters, had a special prayer which he recited before each meeting. It went: 'Dear Lord above, I know thou art the greatest judge of any cricket match that ever takes place. Today two of the most powerful teams oppose each other. If Yorkshire have the best side they will win. And I suppose that if Lancashire have the best side they will win. If the teams are equal or it rains, the game will be drawn. But, Lord, if you leave us to our own devices, we'll hammer them into the ground.'

And so say all true Yorkshiremen! I've a lot of friends on the other side of the Pennines, though, and I am well aware that they think the same, albeit from an exactly opposite point of view. What's more, Yorkshire and Lancashire usually present a common face to outsiders.

Like the man said at a Roses game when a visitor from the south ventured an opinion on the state of the contest: 'It's nothing to do with thee.'

For my own part, I've come to learn that you can achieve more in terms of relationships with a little joke than you can by trying to wield the big stick, and I can honestly say that I've had very few anxious moments out in the middle.

I'm glad to say I can usually see the funny side of most things, although people tell me I look so serious. Not so long ago I appeared on a Radio Two programme called *The Seven Ages of Man*. I didn't think too much about it when I accepted the invitation, but I had a shock when I discovered that it was a series on people approaching their seventies. I've never quite found out why they asked me, but I got some funny looks for a few weeks afterwards. Presumably the BBC must have thought I was past the pensionable age.

As somebody suggested, it could be being so cheerful that keeps me young, and I hope that readers will discover plenty to cheer them in this book.

Dickie Bird, Barnsley, September 1988.

||| 1 |||

World Cup Jamboree

The limited-overs version of the game is not at all popular with many people and in some quarters it simply isn't cricket. I know what the critics mean. There is a certain amount of crash, bang and wallop about the approach. All the same, I have to say that some of my biggest moments have been experienced at this level.

Nothing, for example, can ever compare with that now famous Gillette Cup semi-final between Lancashire and Gloucestershire at Old Trafford, when we finished at 9 pm in total darkness. The players trooped off whistling 'By The Light Of The Silvery Moon,' a tune which became the theme song for that particular match. It's been said often enough that it is impossible to explain cricket to a complete outsider, but I wonder what the Russians would have made of that scene. Thirteen players, two umpires and a packed crowd straining their eyes in the gathering gloom to pick out a small red ball being hurled about and struck with a couple of bits of wood.

The World Cup, too, has become something special – a gathering together of all the cricket-playing nations over a brief, action-packed period in an event that has captured the imagination of millions. This is a great advertisement for the game and I am very proud to have been a part of the first four competitions. I have to admit to one slight disappointment in that I lost my record of having stood in all the finals when, in India in 1987, England and Australia contested the concluding match. That was an interesting occasion, for it was the first time there had been a panel of umpires. In England for the first three World Cups, our own umpires officiated in all games, but in India and Pakistan things were given an even keener international flavour.

For several years there has been a lot of controversy about the standard of umpiring, but it is worth noting that in the whole of the World Cup in India and Pakistan there were no arguments or disputes. I represented England along with David Shepherd, the old – and I use the word in its most respectful sense – Gloucestershire batsman who quickly established himself as a favourite with players and spectators alike when he came onto the first-class umpires' list.

Just for the record the other umpires were David Archer (West Indies), Khalid Aziz (Pakistan), Mehboob Shah (Pakistan), P. W. Vidanagamage (Sri Lanka), Amanullah Khan (Pakistan), Khizer Hyatt (Pakistan), Steve Woodward (New Zealand), V. K. Ramaswamy (India), P. D. Reporter (India), Ram Babu Gupta (India), Tony Crafter (Australia) and D. N. Dotiwata (India). They were a happy band who spent many hours in the middle and possibly nearly as many in the air. Discerning readers will no doubt note the omission of my old friend Shakoor Rana, but more of him later.

I was, of course, very honoured to be chosen, but from the start I had a sinking sensation in the pit of my stomach, which seemed to know what was coming. Dickie Bird is, I can tell you, well known on the circuit for his odd eating habits. I am both a bad traveller and distinctly delicate in matters of digestion. So the thought of touring India and Pakistan with all the heat and the spicy food filled me with dread. I decided to make my will. A lot of cricketers and even more Press men offered a kind of comfort by stressing that arrangements were well in hand for a state funeral, with a procession round Lord's. I even considered taking a crate of baked beans, just to be on the safe side.

These, I was assured, would keep me going. But I have enough trouble packing a small suitcase, so I had to abandon myself to the fates. At home, incidentally, I don't usually have any serious problems, for cricket food is invariably simple and straightforward – chicken salad, beef salad, ham salad, even just salad sometimes. I remember the great Gary Sobers once telling a young professional: 'You can't consider yourself established until you have completed a ton of lettuce in May.'

Some misfortune invariably attaches itself to any trip I undertake and there I stood in my house at Barnsley on the morning of departure checking my luggage for the umpteenth time. I had already packed and unpacked my case until my arms ached, but at last I had convinced myself that nothing had been forgotten. All I required was for the taxi to be on time to get me to the station.

Sure enough, up it rolled, smack on the dot. With it came a big van from Bassett's, the Sheffield-based firm that makes liquorice allsorts, and their generosity caused me a few anxious moments. It turned out that they had read about my fears of foreign food. 'We've been sent with a month's supply of liquorice allsorts, Dickie,' said the driver. 'We don't want you wasting away.' As they handed me a giant-sized box, Yorkshire Television cameras turned up to film my departure. A couple of passing dogs took an interest in the proceedings. The taxi driver, anxious about the time, gave a few toots on the horn and the whole business turned into a pantomime straight out of a Carry On film. It was with a great sigh of relief that I squeezed into the cab and we got away, catching my train with only a few seconds to spare. At least, I thought, I shall get a bit of peace and quiet on the journey. How totally wrong can you be?

Sitting back in my seat watching the comforting English countryside flash past, I decided to sample some of Bassett's wares and was contentedly munching away when the crown came off one of my teeth. Panic set in at once, particularly as I swallowed it in my surprise. There was not a lot I could do about it. My schedule did not allow for a visit to the dentist. In a word, I was powerless. Still, it didn't feel too bad until the flight got under way. Gradually the ache developed and by the time I arrived in India it had reached epic proportions. Things were not exactly helped by the fact that we appeared to fly round the country about three times before finally touching down in Delhi.

For part of the journey we were joined by the West Indian party, and they were in a jolly mood. They reminded me that Malcolm Marshall had given me good advice in the past. He could not do anything about the toothache, but he did help with the potential stomach trouble. 'You listen to me, Dickie,' he once said, 'Get yourself a bottle of Angostura Aromatic Bitters and put some in everything you drink. You'll be as right as rain then, man.' I can tell you, he's right. They did the trick and I still keep a bottle for emergencies in the little cocktail bar in the corner of my cottage.

My first visit in India was to the England camp for a word with the team doctor, Tony Hall. Needless to say, Mike Gatting and his squad thought it very amusing. 'One out, all out, Dickie,' they chorused as word about my missing crown got around. Dr Hall thought I ought to go home. 'You must be joking,' I said. 'I've just flown half-way across the world. I must get it fixed here.' He could not sort out my tooth himself, but had at least part of the answer. 'Get on the bed and drop your trousers,' he instructed, and, with clinical precision, he gave me an injection. 'There, you can go and find a local dentist now,' he told me.

I have to say that I did have real doubts about holding the World Cup in India and Pakistan. I felt they might have difficulty with the organisation. I could not have been more wrong. They did things brilliantly and Mr I. S. Bindra, the secretary of the Indian Board of Control, stepped in very smartly to lend me much-needed assistance. A taxi was summoned, the driver given the essential instructions and off we went. The only thing wrong with Indian taxis is that they lack air conditioning. So, with the pounding in the side of my face and the stifling heat, I had almost passed out when we reached our destination, a dilapidated building that bore little resemblance to the starched white surgeries in England.

It certainly did nothing to raise my very low spirits, but I had no real alternative, so in I went. To say conditions were basic would be very much an understatement. But the dentist, who did not have a waiting list or even a queue, turned out to be a most charming man. He invited me into his chair and promptly set about the offending area with his drill. Within seconds I had literally hit the roof, my reaction as he hit the nerve sending dentist and drill half-way across the room. 'It does seem a bit sensitive,' he admitted as he crawled about on his hands and knees to retrieve the drill from a corner. 'Never mind,' he continued, wiping the drill on his sleeve, 'Indian dentists are the very best in the world, much better than in England, you'll see. I will sort you out very quick.'

After poking about a bit more, the dentist suddenly asked: 'Have you got the crown?' Obviously I hadn't. 'No, I swallowed it,' I explained. 'Yes, but surely you looked for it,' he insisted. It took me some time to convince him that the process would have been far too involved. Obviously a crown for a tooth was quite a valuable item in his part of the world. Mind you, they are not exactly cheap in England and I have since paid £50 for one. So perhaps his thinking was a bit more practical than mine.

To be honest, I didn't suffer any more discomfort and eventually he straightened up. 'Fine now,' he said. 'You

'It does seem a bit sensitive,' he admitted ...

come back tomorrow.' Next day I reported back and, sure enough, he had a crown ready. Unfortunately, it did not fit to his satisfaction. He had no nurse to assist him, but on the second day a small boy was sitting on a box in the corner of the room. The dentist called his name. 'You get on bicycle and hurry,' he told him, adding some complicated instructions in what I can only imagine was the local dialect. About half an hour later the lad returned with the crown adjusted by some Indian dental mechanic. Whatever had been done, it fitted well enough to gain the dentist's approval, and I have to say that it has not given me one second's trouble from that day. It must have been a magnificent job and, as an extra bonus for a good old-fashioned Yorkshireman, the Indian Cricket Board presumably footed the bill, for I never had to pay anything.

As a result, I cheered up a lot and, after a few hours of being very guarded about chewing anything, I completely forgot that I had a crown fitted.

Indeed, I went to a reception in Bangalore in high spirits. In the foyer of the hotel, however, who should I bump into but Geoff Boycott, working as a cricket expert for the *Daily Mail* after retiring the previous season as Yorkshire's opening batsman. 'Just the man I want to see,' he said. 'Come with me and I'll treat you to something to eat. You can't be too careful with your stomach.' This seemed a very good offer and I fully expected to sit down to a gourmet meal, for Geoff is extremely fussy about his diet. Talk about great expectations! I followed him down a corridor to the hotel shop, where he purchased two bars of fruit and nut chocolate – one each. 'I know chocolate is very expensive out here,' he said. 'But this will do you more good than anything. So eat up.'

Well, one of the nuts must have slipped into the bar with its shell intact, because I promptly lost a filling and found myself back with my old friend the dentist next morning. He spent a couple of hours talking about cricket, telling me that India would win the World Cup again, and then put in another filling, which, like the crown, has stood the test of time.

I suppose the dentist must have had other patients, but I never saw anyone else there. He was, though, typical of the Indians, a warm and hospitable people. They also have some of the best hotels. The Taj Mahal in Bombay, the Delhi Taj Palace and the West End in Bangalore are as good as any in which I have stayed. The only trouble was that every time I tried to go for a walk in the street I found myself mobbed by people who just wanted to say 'hello' or wish me well. All the cricketers had the same experience, so we spent a bit of time talking to the locals wherever we went.

Thanks to the advice of Malcolm Marshall and my own cautious approach to food, I did not have an upset stomach at all. I soon settled for safety. Breakfast consisted of two boiled eggs, luncheon was exactly the same, but I relaxed a little at dinner and had two boiled eggs with chips. The other thing I really enjoyed was a kind of Indian bread. The waiters must have been having some sort of bet among themselves, for they came up with the menu each time and tried to persuade me to have curry. They had no chance!

Even so, I did fall ill. I picked up a type of fever, possibly because it was very hot everywhere you went, while the hotels, with their excellent air conditioning, were pleasantly cool. Sometimes the change in temperature hit you like a brick wall. Anyway, I had to go and see Dr Hall again. His room looked like a pharmacy, crammed almost wall to wall with every sort of pill and potion you could imagine. He packed me off to bed and then fell ill himself, getting, as he said, more runs than all the players put together.

David Shepherd also caught the bug, much to the amusement of the waiters. 'You'll get better first, Dickie,' one of them said. 'Much less of you to be poorly.' Shep, of course, is solidly built and his habit of dancing about on one leg when the scoreboard showed either a team or individual total on Nelson made him a great favourite with the spectators, who had no idea, of course, what he was doing. Perhaps some English enthusiasts are not aware of the significance of 111 either, so I'll explain.

Cricketers are by nature a superstitious lot, and they regard 111 as an unlucky number. The Australians have a thing about 87, which is, of course, 13 short of the century mark, but I am not sure just why 111 has become significant in England. The name 'Nelson' is associated because the great admiral had one eye, one arm and, to put the matter as politely as possible, one bottom, and in all dressing rooms the cry goes up at 111. Then everyone present has to lift his feet off the floor until the score moves on. If a wicket falls there is an immediate search for someone who has broken the ritual. As a former player, of course, Shep has long been part of this little tradition and it has followed him into his role as an umpire. He can't, of course, get both feet off the floor, so he does the next best thing and hops up and down.

None of that has anything to do with me being ill, though. I remained in bed with my high temperature, and quite a few of the England players took the trouble to come and visit me, with Allan Lamb popping in and out every few minutes.

Allan is a tremendous practical joker. When England played New Zealand at Trent Bridge in 1983, he caught me out by bringing some jumping crackers onto the field. How he lit them I can't imagine, but as I settled down at the bowler's end for the start of an over he dropped them behind my back and the next moment I was dancing like a dervish while the players fell about in heaps of helpless laughter.

He also had me really hot under the collar at Old

If a wicket falls there is an immediate search for someone who has
broken the ritual.

Trafford when Northamptonshire were involved in a championship clash with Lancashire. We had just finished luncheon on the second day and were having a quiet chat in the umpires' room when I noticed smoke coming under the door.

Jumping up to investigate, I found the door locked. The atmosphere became like an old-fashioned pea-soup fog and we had to force the door to escape. Needless to say, Allan had somehow found a key to fasten us in and then put a couple of smoke bombs against the bottom of the door. We were late on parade and as we hurried to take up our places with the fieldsmen and batsmen already in position we had to take a lot of good-natured ribbing. They reckon that a year later you could still smell smoke in the umpires' room at Lancashire headquarters.

Allan came up at close of play looking genuinely apologetic and said how sorry he was for his little prank. 'No hard feelings about what I have done today, Dickie, I hope,' he said. 'Certainly not, Allan,' I replied, deciding to bluff it out and not let him think he had got the better of us. 'You will have your little joke.' Allan persisted. 'You really aren't angry with me for what I have done today,' he repeated. I should have been more wary, but I fell into the trap. 'Allan, once and for all and in front of witnesses,' I insisted, pointing to the ring of grinning faces, 'you are forgiven.'

'Right then,' he said. 'See you tomorrow, Dickie. Have a good trip home.' When I went out to the car park, however, I found my car on bricks with all four wheels neatly stacked against the side. There was no sign of the culprit, but I am sure I could hear the faint sound of suppressed laughter as I hurried to find the groundsman, who kindly gave me a hand to get mobile again. To add insult to injury, Allan came up next day. 'I slept a lot better last night after you had been such a good sport,' he said.

'I didn't know about my car then,' I shouted, pretending to be really angry. But Allan spread his arms wide in mock surprise and asked: 'What happened to it?' He has never admitted his part in the incident, but I am convinced I had been yet again the victim of his sense of humour.

All this brings me back to India. I felt too poorly to worry about what Allan might be getting up to, and just kept telling him to let me get some rest. In that part of the world they have armed guards on the corridors of the hotels, obviously to protect the guests, so you feel pretty safe – most of the time. I had fallen into a fitful feverish sleep when the door suddenly burst open and several guards marched in under the direction of 'Sergeant-Major' Lamb. 'Right, men,' he ordered, 'Let's put him out of his misery.' At this they levelled their rifles and shouted 'Bang!' in unison as I dived under the bed-clothes.

Fortunately I soon recovered and managed to attend an official dinner, which turned out to be something special with a cleverly arranged menu to mark the festivities. I figured on the list of courses, which was quite a distinction, and the whole thing had a strong cricket connection. It read:

OPENING PAIR

Cross Bat (a delicious prawn, lobster and crabmeat cocktail).
First Slip (cream of celery and leek soup).

ONE DOWN

Light Roller (paupiettes of fish stuffed with
spinach with Nantua sauce).
Dicky Bird (grilled chicken with pimento coulis).
Out for a Duck (roast duck served with sauce
Bigarade).
Straight into the Hams (hamburger topped with
sour cream and scallion dressing).
The Oval (a vegetarian speciality).

TWO DOWN

*Clean Bowled (grilled spicy prawns, marinated in
ginger, garlic green chillies and lemon juice).*
*Fishy Fielders (fish fingers served with tartare
sauce).*
*Leg Before Wicket (three grilled sausages and a
grilled leg of chicken served with mashed potatoes
and a grilled tomato).*
*Bradman's Bat (mutton seekh kebabs,
sandwiched in a bat-shaped roll with chutney and
onion salad).*
Eden Garden (moong dal and fenugreek waffles).

NIGHT WATCHMAN

*Sixer (White wine jelly garnished with diced
fruits).*
Chinaman (vanilla and plum mousse).
Full Toss (chocolate mousse).
*How's That (macedoine of fruits, soaked in white
wine, covered with half strawberry, half pistachio
ice cream).*

No, I am not sure myself what some of the items tasted
like, but I can tell you it was one occasion upon which I
got off my boiled egg diet and spread my wings a bit.

It was just as well that I eventually felt fully fit because
the schedule turned out to be very demanding, as you
might realise from a quick look at my travel plans for the
World Cup. On 1 October I flew from Delhi to Madras,
which took two and a half hours, and I then had the real
luxury of ten days in one place. But after that I began to
feel like a bird of the feathered variety as I winged my
way from place to place. Things got really hectic and my
programme read: 11 October, Madras to Bangalore; 15
October, Bangalore to Bombay; 19 October, Bombay to
Delhi; 23 October, Delhi to Ahmedabad; 27 October,
Ahmedabad to Bombay; 28 October, Bombay to Nagpur.

So there I was, being shuttled to and fro across India

from one ground to another. Without doubt, life was much harder for the organisers than when the World Cup took place in England, for we have a simple motorway system that links the centres – although with traffic jams and road works it is not always easy to clock up the miles as quickly as you would like.

In India and Pakistan, though, flying is essential and there is room for more things to go wrong. My flight from Bombay to Delhi should have taken off at 8.40 in the morning. So I got up at about 4.30, had a bath and packed my things. My taxi turned up safely enough and I got to the airport by 6.00. Nothing happened. I waited around for a while, expecting all the time that someone would let me know what to do. Eventually I made some enquiries, which is not easy, and discovered that no one had remembered to inform me that the departure time had been changed to late afternoon.

I had to go back to the hotel. My room had been cleared and set up for another guest so the only thing to do was sit about and wait, doing my best to get some much-needed sleep. I closed my eyes, but simply could not drop off. So by the time I finally became airborne I was exhausted. Worse followed. A hold-up developed at Delhi, and I had still not cleared the airport by midnight. 'No problem, Mr Dickie, we are looking after you,' they kept telling me, but I had got past caring. The final straw came when at last I reached my destination and the hotel said they had no rooms left. 'Well,' I told the manager, 'If you don't find me a room, there will be no cricket match. You'll be having a funeral instead – mine.'

Mercifully that represented the lowest point. A bed was found and I gratefully collapsed onto it and slept. Normally I suffer a bit from insomnia. I need a lot of peace and quiet and when we are at Lord's, for example, I have an arrangement with the Westmoreland Hotel, just across the road, under which they let me have their quietest room. It would not have mattered in Delhi if they had put a herd of elephants in my room, however. Nothing could have kept me awake.

In passing, I sometimes have a nightmare about falling asleep out in the middle. It's silly, no doubt, but umpires do get very tired on long days and there are a number of funny stories about the odd one dozing in the afternoon sun.

I recall being told about an occasion in the old days at Bramall Lane, Sheffield, where the spectators were as sharp as the city's famous knives. On this particular day, one member of the public had been loudly criticising Yorkshire's efforts in the field as Lancashire put on a lot of runs in a Roses clash. As the score mounted he became more and more agitated and his voice echoed around the ground. Eventually a perspiring Yorkshire bowler got the ball past the bat. More in hope than expectation he appealed for lbw, getting no response from the umpire. 'For heaven's sake give him,' roared the noisy barracker. 'What's the matter, have you gone to sleep?' 'Impossible,' said one of his long-suffering neighbours. 'Nobody could sleep through this racket.'

I had one other unfortunate experience in Madras, where David Shepherd and I were well looked after and given a car with a driver. When we arrived, however, we felt more like taking a gentle walk in the fresh air than a sticky ride, so we enquired about a beach. It was not far away and soon we were walking alongside the water. 'This is the life,' I said, taking in the scenery and feeling very relaxed. Suddenly David pulled me up short. 'Just look at your feet, Dickie,' he cried. We had not been warned that this part of the beach was part of the sewage disposal system for the area – and I had walked in some distinctly unpleasant stuff. The only solution was a quick trip into the sea to wash it off. There I was, fully dressed, paddling almost up to my knees like an overgrown schoolboy. My

I sometimes have a nightmare about falling asleep out in the middle.

quick dip did the trick and we hurried back to the hotel to dry out. Having learned our lesson, we never took the chance of another walk.

You can't have a show without Punch and Shakoor Rana popped up. With a crazy sense of timing, he telephoned me in the middle of the night, his call causing a moment of panic. I could not imagine why anyone should be ringing then. 'I want you to get me a ticket for the World Cup games,' he instructed. 'I am your good friend and you should be able to do this for me.' Half asleep, I could barely understand him. 'You must be able to get all the tickets you want,' I argued. But this turned out not to be the case.

Shakoor came to the hotel and I managed to get him one or two tickets. 'You can come and meet my family,' he invited. 'Sorry,' I said, 'I've such a tight schedule.' I did not want to get involved in any social activities. I intended to rest as much as I could. In fact, the England boys claimed that they were going to buy me a microwave bed to help me to get a few hours of shut-eye in only ten minutes!

'Never mind, Dickie,' decided Shakoor. 'You can meet my family next time you come to visit Pakistan. Perhaps you could give me some more of your white caps, they are worth more than money in my country. He took a couple out of my bag before I could reply, and I haven't seen him since, although he has been very much in the headlines. I call him the Sergeant-Major and that's how I shall always remember him.

All too soon the great adventure came to an end. Australia won the World Cup and England finished gallant runners-up in an exciting final which I know many people watched on television back home in England. Shep and I travelled on the return journey with Geoff Boycott, who received a lot of attention from the Press, being romantically linked with a young lady. All I can say is that he sat with us and enjoyed a brief moment of anonymity on the aeroplane.

The pilot must have been told we were on board, for he came up and invited me onto the flight deck to talk about cricket. 'You know Geoff Boycott is sitting back there,' I told him, but he shrugged his shoulders. 'I am an attacking batsman myself,' he said, proving the point with some dashing imaginery strokes. 'I'd rather you kept your hands on the steering wheel,' I said, at which he roared with laughter. 'You are very safe with me,' he cried, 'much safer than the bowlers, I can tell you.' He must be one of the very few batsmen who think they are better than 'Boycs', who sublimely slept through all this.

On a slightly more serious note, I thought all the World Cup cricket that I saw was very good. Some of the games maintained a very high standard indeed, with outstanding athleticism from nearly everyone taking part. The days have certainly gone when the more ponderous members of any side could 'hide' in the field or when key batsmen and bowlers could be allowed the luxury of strolling about.

Bill Bowes, one of the tremendous cricketing personalities we shall talk about more than once, became the target for some criticisms early in his career because of his fielding. He did not race after the ball in the hope of turning four into three. He had to save his energies for the serious business of fast bowling and received instructions not to waste his efforts. In addition, partners often ran him out for the same reason. Batting too long might sap his energy!

One very interesting point emerged. Nineteen of the twenty-seven games in the World Cup were won by the side batting first – a statistic which no doubt interested a lot of English county captains. As tactical awareness developed in limited-overs competitions, it had been widely felt that chasing rather than setting a target offered some advantage. The World Cup suggested otherwise.

I suppose W. G. Grace gave the best advice when asked about what to do when winning the toss. 'If it is a good pitch, I bat,' he said. 'If it looks as though there might be a little help for the bowlers, I think about it for a bit and then I bat. If there looks likely to be a lot of help for the bowlers, I think about it a bit longer and then I bat.' I also recall a famous bowler expressing his disgust when asked by his captain about the possibility of putting in the opposition: 'Well, if tha does, I hope tha'll bowl 'em out – because I shan't.'

Scotland decided to field first against Yorkshire in the Benson and Hedges Cup tie at Headingley in May 1986, and they conceded 317 runs in the 55 overs while claiming five wickets. 'Well, at least we know how many we have to get to win,' suggested one official, seeking to restore morale. 'Aye,' observed another, 'a damned sight too many.'

In reaching the World Cup final, England did better than most of their critics expected and Mike Gatting and his boys showed lots of character and spirit. I desperately wanted them to beat Australia in the final, which I could approach purely as a spectator. All the same, I have to admit to a sneaking feeling of disappointment when I could not umpire the big game, for I had taken part in the three previous finals. Still, you can't have everything and at least I was part of the show.

||| 2 |||

On the Road, In the Air

As every schoolboy knows, Admiral Nelson, the greatest of our heroes at sea, was a poor sailor and endured bouts of sickness every time his ship left port. I can look back to his suffering with a good deal of sympathy. Despite visiting most of the far-slung corners of the globe, I am not a good traveller. I worry too much and always have the fear of something going wrong. Actually it often does!

I still have far from fond memories of being talked into a trip on Peasholm Park Lake at Scarborough by Don Wilson when we were both members of the Yorkshire team enjoying a few days of relaxed cricket at the seaside town's famous festival. It did not seem like a good idea, even at the time, but reluctantly I got into a little rowing boat and Don cheerfully sent us skimming across the water. There were, of course, a lot of holiday-makers with their children doing the same thing, so we were part of a happy, crowded scene. Within a few minutes, however, I began to feel sea-sick, even though there was hardly a ripple on the water.

'It's no use, Don, you'll have to get me back on dry land,' I pleaded, but he just carried on enjoying himself. There was nothing for it – I climbed out of the boat and waded ashore. Fortunately the lake is no more than a couple of feet deep, but I must have looked silly struggling through the water and trying to avoid all the boats. I didn't care, though, and anyone who has been sea-sick will understand just why. In the circumstances, it is a good

There was nothing for it – I climbed out of the boat and waded ashore.

job cricketers do not have to travel by ship these days, so I am not put under much pressure in this direction. But I dread to think what I would have been like going to Australia in the old days, when the touring party was at sea for about six weeks.

I would have done anything to play for England, of course. But whether I could have survived such a trip is a different matter. Ray Illingworth is another who has found difficulty coping with the thousands of miles that he has travelled during a long career as player and now broadcaster. Ray can be car-sick almost before he gets out of his drive. A few years ago he was invited to be one of the personalities on a cricket cruise organised by the *Cricketer* magazine on the *Canberra*. He had some doubts about the venture and these turned into a dreadful reality in the Bay of Biscay, which is often very rough. Ray didn't show his face for two days and told me: 'Dickie, I thought of you in Scarborough and wondered about walking home, but I felt the water might have been a bit too deep.'

A lot of the old-timers used to enjoy the Australian tour, however. Although it covered most of the winter and kept them away from their families, they got a good rest going and coming back. The modern stars such as Ian Botham and David Gower, who are in almost constant action year in year out, with quick aeroplane journeys making it possible to fit in more and more Tests and one-day internationals, have often said how much they would have liked to have had the benefit of a long, slow sea trip.

The Press men had a good time as well, with little or nothing to write about. It was more like a well-paid six-week holiday. One newspaper received just two words in almost two months from the man they had sent to cover Freddie Brown's trip down under in 1950–51 – a telegram which read simply: 'Land sighted.'

To balance this, it seems to me that there must have been periods when the routine at sea became a bit boring, especially for a group of young men without their wives and girlfriends. Cruise liners, of course, make sure that there is a wide range of entertainment available, but this was not really the case when cricketers ploughed through the waves en route to Australia.

On one voyage, however, I am reliably informed that the ship's owners thoughtfully provided a conjuror to entertain in the main lounge during the evenings. They no doubt felt that he would be something of a novelty, and he began to go through his repertoire of tricks and illusions as soon as they slipped anchor and got under way.

It so happened that the ship had a semi-official mascot in the shape of a parrot of above-average intelligence which lived permanently in the lounge. It did not take long for the bird to join in the fun. After a couple of nights it decided to provide a running commentary on the conjuror's tricks. When he produced a bunch of flowers from thin air it shouted: 'They were up his sleeve!' When he made a lighted cigarette appear and disappear, the wretched bird ruined the whole business by revealing: 'It's behind his hand!'

Somehow the conjuror managed to keep his hands from the parrot's neck, but there was no doubt his standing had slumped alarmingly when, just as he was attempting the most complicated and difficult trick he knew, something went wrong in the boiler room and the ship blew up. The tremendous explosion sent everything into the air and when the debris settled on the sea there was hardly anything to be seen. By chance the parrot and the conjuror discovered themselves on the same bit of wreckage, where they remained companions for several days, tossed about in the ocean swell. Finally, the bird broke the long silence. 'All right, I give up,' it admitted. 'How did you make the ship disappear?'

Cricket and travel, of course, have always been linked, and when the English have gone abroad they have taken their best-loved game with them. As a result cricket has flourished in many places, thanks to the efforts of men with more enthusiasm than skill. Some have been missionaries, the muscular arm of the church, who introduced sport as well as religion to the outposts of civilisation. That cannot have been easy and I have always enjoyed an admittedly far-fetched yarn about a reverend gentleman somewhere in deepest Africa who, as soon as he arrived, decided to teach the natives how to play.

Watched by a polite and very interested gathering of locals, he carefully cut some branches to the right length to make six stumps. He had, of course, taken a bat and cricket ball with him as a part of his essential luggage. Next he carefully paced out the ritual twenty-two yards in a small clearing at the edge of the village and then he smoothed out the ground as best he could to create a rough and ready pitch.

Gathering the natives around him, with the aid of an interpreter who had some slight grasp of English, he slowly and with a good deal of repetition explained all the laws. This took a long time. But he was much encouraged by the fact that his lecture was punctuated by great shouts of 'Ungali!' from his audience, who were laughing and shouting and obviously deriving great pleasure from his words. Sadly as he reached the end of his lesson the light was fading. With due regard to long-established tradition, he told the natives they would have to wait until next day to actually put theory into practice. 'Ungali,' they all roared as they departed back to their huts, leaving the missionary with his interpreter. As this pair made their way back along the trail to the missionary's hut they came across evidence of the recent presence of elephants in the shape of droppings. 'Oh, do be careful,' said the interpreter, 'or you will step in the ungali.'

As you may have gathered, one of the major problems in operating overseas is the food. A change of diet can be disastrous, especially when the strange food is hot and spicy, and there are literally hundreds of stomach-churning accounts of misadventures in India. Alf Gover, the Surrey and England fast bowler, reputedly suffered considerable misfortune on a private tour to that country. He became ill during his opening spell with the new ball and in the course of his run-up realised that drastic emergency action was needed. Instead of releasing the ball, he continued on his way down the pitch, passed the startled batsman and continued over the outfield with ever-increasing pace. He disappeared into the pavilion and within a minute or two the sounds of the primitive plumbing system could be heard. Alf did not reappear, however, and after some delay the captain hurried to find out exactly what was happening.

As he reached the dressing room he called out: 'Gover, Gover, where are you?' From the toilet area came a weak voice. 'I am sorry, sir, but I am too ill to continue.' 'Oh very well, then,' said the captain. 'But you had better let me have the ball back.'

The early pioneers undoubtedly had a lot of courage, for they were going very much into the unknown when they left their little villages to visit Australia. They did not even have the advantage of luxury liners and I wonder what the basic uncomfortable-looking ships were like in the 1800s. Men in general were very sturdy, though, in what was a more demanding era and those from Yorkshire were not easily impressed. Tom Emmett, George Ulyett and Ephraim Lockwood were three of the best cricketers of their generation and they went to America with a representative side. Lockwood, so the legend goes, saw nothing special in the majesty of the Niagara Falls. 'This is a sight worth seeing, isn't it?' the wicketkeeper George Pinder is supposed to have asked. 'Nay, I make nowt of it. I'd sooner be at home in Lascelles Hall,' replied Lockwood. Another member of that little party is reputed to have added: 'What's good about it? There's nowt to stop t'water.'

Lascelles Hall, for those who may not be familiar with Yorkshire and its history, is a little hamlet just outside Huddersfield which played a dominant role in the development of the county team. Those who live there regard it as the centre of the sporting universe and assume the whole world is well aware of its location. Thus during the war a Lascelles Hall inhabitant, stationed near London, came before the magistrates on a drunk and disorderly charge. 'Where do you come from,' asked the bench. 'Lascelles Hall,' came the reply. 'And where might that be?' 'Well, if you're going from Huddersfield to Wakefield tha turns left at t'big chimney,' was the answer.

Closer to home, I am always surprised that we do not have, in terms of sponsorship, the Motorway Maintenance Sunday League or the Tarmacadam County Championship. It is not that I do not admire the business organisations that have so generously supported our first-class game, but somehow it is the road network that seems most closely linked with top level cricket. We spend many hours hurrying from one venue to the next because it is simply not possible to fit all the teams into a neat and accommodating programme.

Take Yorkshire at the 1987 Benson and Hedges Cup final, for example. As one of the umpires for the match against Northamptonshire, I had first-hand knowledge of the problems they could face if it rained on the big day. Yorkshire had to fulfil a Sunday League date with Middlesex up at Scarborough on the day after the final, so if the cup tie had spread over into the Monday, Phil Carrick and his boys would have faced two tremendous journeys while under a lot of pressure on the field. Can you imagine Manchester United nipping back to Old Trafford at half-time in an FA Cup Final to play a league game before dashing back to Wembley to complete the more important business?

I would not say cricketers think nothing about it, but they readily accept a much harder life than most other sportsmen. During the 1984 summer, Yorkshire had to travel from Middlesbrough to Hove for a Benson and Hedges Cup quarter-final and faced the prospect of arriving on the south coast in the small hours of the morning. Not surprisingly the team had the prayer mats out and were delighted when heavy rain in the North-East washed out the last day of their championship clash with Somerset, enabling them to reach Hove in time for a good night's sleep. Yes, they did win the cup tie.

Middlesbrough was the scene of another waterlogged finish two year earlier, when I was on duty with Jack van Geloven. Yorkshire's match with Northamptonshire marked the end of Chris Old's run as captain and on the Monday the news broke that Ray Illingworth was to return as captain. Illy had been team manager but, even though he was then 50 years of age, the county felt he could help bring the side along better by putting on his whites again and getting onto the field.

Yorkshire faced another long haul south, that time to Ilford to meet Essex, so they were not sorry then when it rained on the last day. Jack and I had to observe the regulations, however, and the ground was not wet enough to abandon play before the luncheon interval. I had to admit that there seemed no hope at all of play, but we simply had to wait. In the early afternoon, with rain pouring down, things had clearly taken a turn for the worse, so I thought we could go out and inspect the square.

The dressing rooms at Middlesbrough back onto a big, football-type bath – the cricket club share's facilities with the Rugby Union club – and we had to pass it on our way from the umpires' room. I have no idea how it happened, but Jack tripped over Graham Stevenson, the Yorkshire and England seam bowler, and fell into the bath, which was full at the time. All concerned thought it very funny, but Jack merely said: 'Don't worry about it, Stevo, by the time I've been out there it will not make any difference.' He was quite right. To do our job properly we did go right onto the square. By the time we had abandoned the match and got back to the shelter of the pavilion it was difficult, if not impossible, to guess which of us had been in the bath. We spent most of the afternoon drying our clothing while the players hurried on to the next engagement.

Another point about cricket is that players and umpires usually drive themselves up and down the country. The costs and the inconvenience make it impossible in most cases to follow the lead of soccer and have coaches. Geoff Boycott is always telling me that if he had not been the world's best batsman he might easily have emerged as the formula one Grand Prix champion and there is no doubt that 'Fiery' can knock up the miles a shade quicker than he collected his runs. In fact, in his earlier days you could easily tell which was his car in the car park. It was the one with the St Christopher on front covering his eyes. David Bairstow is another high-quality driver and if we are going in the same direction he often shouts: 'If you're in a hurry, Dickie, I'll give you a tow.'

One time I could have done with some help was August 1986. I had to drive down to Weston-super-Mare for the championship game between Somerset and Worcestershire. It is nearly all motorway, so in one sense it is not too bad, but I must have settled into a funny driving position. When I eventually got to Weston-super-Mare I simply could not get out of the car. My left leg had locked completely and I had to be lifted out just like a child.

Gradually I got some use back in the limb, but the pain began to drive me absolutely crazy. I managed to get through the first day with John Hampshire, but on the second I had to admit defeat. I struggled to concentrate,

'Don't worry about it Stevo, by the time I've been out there it will not make any difference.

hobbling about from end to end. But the only sensible course was to pull out, making way for Alan Whitehead who turned up to take over. Even then, I took ages to get home. Talk about a bird with one wing!

It is absolutely vital to have reliable transport. You can't afford to lose time breaking down. When I first got onto the umpires' list I had a rather ancient Morris Minor. This never actually let me down, but there were some hairy moments when I thought it might conk out altogether. Eventually, a smooth car salesman who spent a bit of time on the circuit offered to do me a 'very good deal', and I soon became the owner of a new vehicle. At least, it was new to me and came with an impressive pedigree. I set out, therefore, full of confidence, got about twenty miles down the M1 and the engine dropped out. You will probably not be surprised to learn that my salesman 'friend' did not appear after that. I later discovered that one or two other people had been similarly 'caught out'.

Cricket, as I have said, does not lend itself to coach travel. In the first place a county side can be on the road without a break for more than a week, during which they may want to change the team, while the expense would be very high through having to keep the driver and his vehicle on hand. Yorkshire did, however, have one for their long journey to Perth for a Benson and Hedges Cup qualifying clash with Scotland in 1984. That was the tie in which we had two tea intervals because letters from Lord's informing us of a change in the regulations did not reach the other umpire John Holder and myself in time.

The county kindly allowed us to travel with the team and return to Leeds with them on the Sunday morning. We made leisurely progress south during the morning and, as we approached the border, the general cry went up for a refreshment stop. There are strictly limited facilities north of the border on the Sabbath, but eventually we came across a small country-style hotel. Our hopes were dashed when we saw a notice which read 'No coach parties,' but Geoff Boycott and David Bairstow volunteered to lead an expeditionary force and I joined them.

We entered the hotel, which was empty, and were met by the man in charge. 'I'm Geoff Boycott, the England batsman, this is David Bairstow, the Yorkshire captain, and this is Dickie Bird, the famous umpire,' said Geoff. 'We are on our way home after playing Scotland and would like to stop for some food.' The man looked us up and down and moved to the door. 'I don't care who you are,' he retorted. 'That's my sign, that's a bus and you'd better get on your way. I don't serve coach parties so I wouldn't serve you even if you were proper sportsmen and played football.' How are the mighty fallen!

I nearly got caught out nearer home. We had, incidentally, managed to get a cup of tea once we got back into England, and, as the landmarks became more familiar, Yorkshire captain Phil Carrick upheld a long-standing tradition of coach trips by taking round the hat for the driver. All of us chipped in, of course, but Boycott was fast asleep, stretched out alongside me. 'We won't wake him up,' decided Carrick, 'You can put a couple of quid in for him, Dickie.' Well, I might be a lot of things, but, as a good Yorkshireman I am not silly with my money. 'You've got to be joking,' I said. 'There's no way he'll believe I've contributed for him, and if he does, he'll want a receipt.' Phil settled for asking 'Fiery' when the coach reached Headingley, but I did not wait to find out if he was as good as his word.

Despite everything, I have to admit that we are comparatively spoiled these days. It is not all that long ago that the hours of play had to be arranged around the railway timetables and Yorkshire undertook the long southern tour of several fixtures simply because they could not get about as easily as we do today. Ted Lester, formerly a hard-hitting batsman with Yorkshire and now their knowledgeable scorer. has always lived in Scarborough. This meant he had a lot further to travel than his colleagues and he used to keep a bicycle at York station. This enabled him to get home when otherwise he would have had no hope. He also cycled the forty-odd miles back the next morning to catch a train.

Things were even harder before the turn of the century when the All England Eleven toured about, struggling, for example, from London to Glasgow during the night to be ready for action next morning. To them even the most uncomfortable train would have been a luxury, and there is an amusing story told about George Anderson, one of the true giants of the distant past.

George was born in Bedale in 1826, so you can guess what life was like for him. Once the All England Eleven had to get from Wisbech to Sleaford by stage coach. The trip involved no great distance, but it was a dark night and the driver got lost. There they were bouncing about the dark Lincolnshire lanes with absolutely no idea which way to go. As someone who relies a lot on road signs, I can imagine how frustrated they must have got. Eventually they came across a sign-post, but with no light they could not read the weatherworn lettering on the arms. One of the team had to be helped to climb up. He struck a match and, after a couple of unsuccessful attempts, discovered the correct road. Even then, the party did not reach their destination until six in the morning – and they were on the field at noon.

As Anderson is reported to have said: 'I have had to play in London on the Wednesday night and in Glasgow the next morning. Was there any wonder I had to be roused from my sleep to go out to bat?'

Talking of the unexpected adventures that can befall a cricketer reminds me of another story from a gentler age. It concerns an amateur batsman who saved money by hitch-hiking from one ground to another and had the opportunity to do so because the programme was nothing like as crowded as it is now. He needed to get from Liverpool across into Yorkshire and had a few days at his disposal, so it looked like a stroke of good fortune when he came across a bargeman in a hostelry. After sharing a convivial glass or two they struck up a passing friendship and the bargeowner, who was going in the right direction, agreed to take the cricketer with him.

Off they went, drifting happily along. The canal was regulated by a series of locks at which the bargee had to declare his cargo. The cricketer took no particular notice of the little ritual, contentedly sitting back and taking in the sun, until gradually the words sank into his subconscious. 'Sixty bags of manure, two dead goats and a cricketer,' sang out the bargee. A repeat performance came at the next lock. 'Sixty bags of manure, two dead goats and a cricketer.' At this point the cricketer decided that pride was at stake. 'Look here, old chap,' he said, 'I'm very grateful for the lift, but I think we shall have to do something about the batting order.'

It is possible that I can claim something of a record for once covering 46,000 miles in four weeks on a sponsored lecture and coaching tour around the world. I had an interesting insight into how some people look at these things one day when I caught the train to London for a meeting at Lord's. I had made myself comfortable in the Edinburgh to London express when the guard came along for the tickets. He checked mine and disappeared back into the corridor, but the door had hardly shut when he reappeared. 'You're Dickie Bird, the Test umpire, aren't you?' 'That's me,' I admitted. He sat down in the next seat and began asking all sorts of questions. I never mind chatting to enthusiasts unless I am very tired, because I will talk to anyone who likes cricket and is interested in the background. I told him all about the sort of life players and umpires live and mentioned my own tour. In turn he informed me that he spent every working day on the Edinburgh to London train, walking up and down the corridor checking tickets. 'It can get a bit boring,' he admitted. 'But I wouldn't want your job. I couldn't cope with all that travelling!'

In one way, I suppose, he was covering a lot of miles, getting nowhere and seeing nothing but the same old scene hurrying past the windows. In one sense, therefore, he might just as well have filled his days strolling up and down the road outside his home. In a similar way, I understand that some of the top pop stars tour around one country after another, spending all their time in the various hotels and dressing rooms along the way. In their case, one place is much the same as another.

At least I can see the sights, even if now and again I do attract a bit of attention. Take Colombo, for example. That is a city where you can have a bit of trouble with the local rules about driving. There is no generally accepted system that I have noticed and it's mostly just a case of every man for himself as the traffic fights for space on the roads. Not even Barnsley in the rush hour offers such a challenge!

In the middle of all the hustle and bustle one day I got a bit lost, so it seemed like a good idea to get out and ask some directions. Unfortunately everyone else stopped as well, creating a real old-fashioned jam. Immediately all the locals were rushing up and shouting: 'Mister Dickie Bird, Mister Dickie Bird, let's see you do some umpiring.' On the spur of the moment, I signalled four byes in the hope of getting things moving again. They may take it for a traffic signal, I thought. That brought a huge cheer.

Next I indicated a six. No-one moved. Finally I gave a stranded auto-rickshaw out with a grand gesture. 'That's out, obstructing the road,' I informed him. All that remained was for me to sign a few autographs and get the directions I needed.

On the spur of the moment, I signalled four byes in the hope of getting things moving again.

I was out there once again in company with the redoubt-able David Shepherd. 'Didn't you once used to be a vicar or something?' he was politely asked. 'No, that was my father,' he replied, keeping his face very straight. We were neutral umpires for some games between Sri Lanka and Pakistan in the Asia Cup and we enjoyed the unusual experience of having some of our decisions wildly cheered by the spectators.

We did run into a spot of bother, though. I gave Asantha de Mel, the Sri Lankan, out caught at the wicket and he made something of a meal of rubbing his arm as he departed. I took no notice, for I knew he had got an edge, but next morning I had a terrible shock.

The local paper arrived carrying a huge headline claim-ing Shep and I had already left for home. 'English umpires Dickie Bird and David Shepherd flew back home last night following complaints about the controversial dismissal of de Mel in yesterday's match. The English umpires were brought down to the Asia Cup to avert controversial umpiring decisions. The local umpires' union boss Upali Mahanama said: "My lips are sealed." '

Apparently this caused tremendous waves throughout Colombo and Tony Lewis, the former Glamorgan and England captain, now a well-known writer and broad-caster, who was working out there, found himself deluged with enquiries. Why, people demanded, were we upset? Could not the Reverend Shepherd have persuaded me to stay? Tony had no answers.

Meanwhile, I sat in my hotel room fuming. I had no doubts about the decision and it had not been seriously queried. In any case, why should it say we have flown home when I was still there?

For the umpteenth time I picked up the paper. Then, I noticed something which puzzled me even more. It con-tained a picture of the Indian team with a caption which indicated that it had been taken as they arrived in Sri

Lanka. I was well aware that they had withdrawn from the competition, so that set me thinking. Calming down I studied the page more closely and my attention fell on another picture. This showed one of the more famous players chasing a streaker across the pitch.

I had just begun to wonder if I was suffering from a touch of the sun when I got a telephone call from the paper's editor. 'What is happening?' I snapped. 'Am I going mad or are you?' 'Don't get too excited, Dickie,' he replied. 'Just take a look at the date.' There is was – Tuesday, April 1!

Despite being the victim of this practical joke, I have the happiest memories of Sri Lanka. Television covered a lot of the cricket and they are so keen out there that I found myself a celebrity. Doors were always open to me and I even managed to get through immigration under the stern gaze of a row of poker-faced officials by merely smiling and saying: 'Mister Dickie Bird, Mister Dickie Bird.' The words were better than my passport.

I even survived a totally unexpected downpour when I moved on to Sharjah. I imagined I would be free from all those difficulties with the weather when I agreed to go out to Sri Lanka, for I had a mental picture of a land of endless bright sunshine filling every single day. Perhaps a telephone call before I left Barnsley should have warned me that this would not be the case.

It came from the Sri Lankan Cricket Board of Control and my immediate reaction was that they were confirming the arrangements for my journey. The voice at the other end said, however: 'Oh, don't give your tickets another thought. They are not important. We will make sure you get here. We know you are the expert on all the bad light. Please remember to bring with you all the light meters you can carry. These are most vital, so do not be forgetting them. We want to have the answer to bad light, so your trip is most urgent.'

You can't take a call like that lightly, so I stuffed a load into my case. But that was by no means the end of the matter.

Hardly had I arrived in Sharjah than the rains came – the first in that part of the world for five years. I got one or two funny stares and the ground had a familiar look, for they managed to find some covers from somewhere and get them on the square, although they were fairly primitive.

Making up for lost time, the weather took a distinct turn for the worse. A torrential downpour steadily gathered momentum until you could hardly see a hand in front of your face or hear yourself shout for help. I certainly needed some.

I was staying in the Continental Hotel, one of the most luxurious in the world, but this was the first rain to fall since it had been built and the water got through everywhere. Outside all the roads were flooded because the drains could not cope and the situation became chaotic. Inside, things were not a lot better. The builder may have been all right in his way, but he had not allowed for the occasional storm. I tried to get a bit of sleep, dozed off and awoke to find about a foot of water sloshing around my bedroom. Eventually the manager turned up and carried me out in his arms to find a bit of drier ground in another room. Somehow, it all reminded me of Peasholm Park once more.

||| 3 |||

United We Stand

Umpires have been the subject of good-natured jocularity ever since the day some anonymous wit first told the joke about the batsmen walking sadly away from the crease and saying to the umpire: 'That wasn't out, you know.' The official, of course, replied: 'Look in the paper tomorrow.' That is the oldest chestnut in the business, even though an attempt was made to update it by giving the batsman the last word, adding: 'It will say I wasn't out – I am the editor.'

All of us who slip on the white coat of officialdom have been assailed by variations of the old, old theme, right down to village green level, where the batting side can be called upon to provide at least one umpire to stand at square leg.

There have, though, been many more stories, some of the least believable being true. One of these inevitably concerned Ray East, a persistent joker who enlivened the most serious situations with his bubbling sense of humour. Jack van Geloven gave him out lbw to the last ball before the tea interval in a championship match and all the way back to the pavilion Easty kept trying to persuade him to change his mind. 'You couldn't really give me out,' he pleaded. 'That ball would not have hit another set of stumps.' Jack remained unmoved. 'Ray, you are out and that's that,' he insisted.

When play resumed, the 'new' Essex batsman came out wearing a big helmet. This caused some surprise since the

'That wasn't out you know.'

spinners were on and the afternoon had become distinctly sticky. The bowler had almost got into his delivery stride before Jack realised what was going on. 'East!' he shouted. 'You've been out once and you can't have another innings.' Ray had to go, sadly dragging himself off again, pausing every few steps to look beseechingly back at Jack. I can't say whether he would have let the bowler deliver the ball, but he got pretty close and his Essex colleagues were doubled up in mirth.

Perhaps Ray East had heard about Tom Emmett, of Yorkshire, way back in 1878. As I understand it, Tom was playing for England against Gloucestershire and facing a lob bowler. By all accounts Tom fancied his chances, but decided to take some care with the first ball which he allowed to pass without offering a stroke. It may have hit a bump or some mark on the pitch, for it moved in and shattered Tom's stumps, much to his embarrassment. He obviously felt very silly being bowled by a ball he had left alone. To cover his confusion, he put the bails back on and took guard again, calling to the triumphant bowler: 'Just let me have that one again, will you.' He departed after this little pantomine, and when he reached the pavilion a spectator approached him, anxious to discover why he had been so easily outwitted.

'Tom, how on earth did that happen?' he asked. 'Don't call me Tom,' came the curt answer. Not to be put off, the spectator persisted: 'Mr Emmett, how did it happen?' 'Don't call me Mr Emmett either,' was the angry response. 'Then what shall I call you?' 'You can call me a damned fool.'

No doubt local league umpires have more back-chat to contend with than we do on the county circuit, although the great Alec Skelding had his leg pulled by the 1948 Australians after he had given out Sid Barnes in what they thought was a poor decision at Grace Road, Leicester. Alec received a note from the tourists suggesting that next day he make sure he had both his white stick and his guide dog with him. Sure enough, Alec did turn up with a stout stick, but he sent a message back to say he regretted that dogs were not allowed into the ground.

Alec also wore glasses and he added that he possessed three pairs – one for sixes, one for leg-byes and one for lbw decisions. Later in the tour Skelding umpired Surrey v Australia at the Oval, where a stray dog ran onto the pitch. Quick as a flash Barnes collected the animal and took it up to Alec saying: 'Here you are at last, Alec, I thought you said they wouldn't let your dog in.' 'It's not mine. I got rid of him for yapping, the same as I'll do with you,' said Alec, having the last word.

Alec, incidentally, liked the odd drink at- the close of play. Having remained until closing time in the local pub one night, he set off for home in the wrong direction and instead of going through the door finished up in the telephone booth. After a few seconds be reappeared. 'I've had an inspection and it's much too dark in there for play,' he said.

He was definitely an eccentric. Bill Bowes became very friendly with him and the two would spend the odd evening together whenever their paths crossed. Bill used to tell of once being taken by Alec to a pub in the Leicester area which contained some decidedly rough characters. Even Bill, a very big, strongly-built man, felt a bit uneasy. 'Don't worry, you'll be all right with me,' Alec assured him. They had a couple of beers and Bill had begun to feel very much at home when suddenly the door burst open and three real bruisers marched in. They gazed around the room and pounced on one of the customers, who gave himself away by trying to crawl under a bench seat. Dragging him kicking and squealing over to the open fire place, they pushed him head first up the chimney, leaving him with his legs dangling over the flames, which quickly roasted his bottom. As soon as they had disappeared the poor victim was rescued. It turned out he owed the local bookmaker money, but Alec sat through it all without turning a hair. 'I often come here for the floor show,' he said to Bill, who was still getting his breath back.

Most of the players called Alec 'Doctor,' at least when he was out of earshot, because he carried his white boots in a medical type of bag. He remained universally popular, right or wrong. 'And that, gentlemen, concludes the entertainment for the day,' he said without fail as he removed the bails at the close of play. He had, in fact, a wonderful rapport with all and sundry, although he could be cutting with his off-the-cuff asides. Like most of us, he suffered disputes with the scoreboard which can lose track of things, and once he marched down to the board in a county match and gave three halfpennies to one of the operators. 'Here, go and get a paper and let's all find out what the total is,' he said.

Almost as celebrated was Bill Reeve, another umpire who loved the game and added character to the proceedings. He crossed swords with Walter Robins, a fiery personality who captained Middlesex and became a very important figure at Lord's as an administrator. 'Cock' Robins – his nickname stemmed from his perky bearing and far from retiring nature – spent a fruitless afternoon wheeling away with his leg-spinners for Middlesex, appealing for a variety of dismissals but without success. On and on he bowled, unchanged from one end through from luncheon to tea, at which stage Bill Reeve handed him back his sweater. The Middlesex sweater, of course, has three scimitars proudly displayed on the front and Robins, refusing to take his, snapped: 'You can stick that up your backside, swords and all.'

George Macaulay, another bowler who never troubled to keep his temper under too tight control, ran into a stonewall of Bill's refusal to give a batsman out. All his passion and his pleading were wasted as Bill continued to say 'not out' in a firm voice. At the close, as they walked off side by side, Bill said: 'You know, George, I reckon only Dr Barnardo's makes more appeals than you.'

Skelding and Reeve were the umpires in 1938 when Yorkshire played a historic match against the Australians at Bramall Lane – a contest that has been the subject of hours of debate after ending in a draw. This was no tame draw. Yorkshire, chasing 150 to win, were 83 for three when rain ended their hopes of a famous victory. Yorkshire were, without any question, a very good side in that season and the fixture drew 35,000 spectators on the first day. Brian Sellers, their bluff, no-nonsense captain, put in the tourists when he won the toss and his attack removed them for 222 on a helpful pitch.

The backbone of the Australian effort was provided by Don Bradman with 59, and Lindsay Hassett with 94. Hassett, on his first tour of England, chipped in with an innings of the highest quality, mixing careful defence with well-judged aggression as he struck three sixes and twelve fours. He appeared certain to reach his century when he was given out lbw by Reeve to Hedley Verity. 'That must have been a close decision,' he ventured later, no doubt disappointed at the outcome. 'Very close,' acknowledged Reeve, adding as he pointed to the departing crowd. 'But I'd rather upset one Australian than thousands of Yorkshiremen, so you had to go.'

I am told that in the Australian second innings Bill Bowes bowled one of the finest spells of all time, beating Bradman with six successive balls in an over. At the end of it, Bradman, in a rare gesture, handed his bat to Sellers. 'Would you like to have a go?' he enquired. 'I can't make anything of him.' Sellers declined the invitation. 'If you think I'm going to show you how to play Bill, you are mistaken,' he said. I don't suppose he was joking, either.

One of the most forceful and engaging personalities in my experience of first-class cricket was Wilf Wooller, who poured so much of his energy into Glamorgan but also served Wales with success as a Rugby Union footballer. There were no half-measures with Wilf, who once offered to give all the spectators their money back because Brian Close had batted on too long in his opinion in a championship fixture. Yorkshire won that game, but Wooller did not concede anything because of a little matter like that.

Fielding at mid-off, fairly wide, he took it upon himself to query a decision by Frank Lee in a championship match, arguing that a not out verdict had been too much in favour of the batsman. He persisted for some time without having any effect on Frank. Eventually Wooller came in to bat in the Glamorgan innings and asked Frank for his normal guard. Frank turned and walked slowly out to wide mid-off. 'I suppose you would like your guard from here,' he said. 'I am reliably informed it's the best place to see what's going on.'

There are different pressures on umpires who operate on the village green or in the casual friendly match. They have other priorities, not always associated with the game itself, and it has to be remembered that they are invested with considerable authority, however brief. Although volunteers are preferred, there are many pressed into service and, while they may be ill equipped in terms of expertise and familiarity with the laws, they possess one decisive virtue. They are available.

The famous broadcaster Gilbert Harding, as a schoolboy, gave the sports master out lbw in the 90s after being instructed to umpire a Teachers v Pupils match, doing so, he claimed, as an act of revenge for having what might have been a nice afternoon ruined.

Another illustration is provided by the description of the country house fixture in which the butler had to stand in when the expected arbiters failed to appear. He had no great interest in cricket, and therefore no deep knowledge of the finer points. As a fair-minded man, he resolved to give everybody not out so that at least any errors ought to balance out. Events were proceeding smoothly when his employer, a keen if limited batsman, set out in pursuit of a short single. The man in the covers swooped with unexpected agility and threw down the stumps at the bowler's end. A great shout arose, demanding the wicket and putting the butler in something of a quandary. Pausing only momentarily, he drew himself to his full height and intoned: 'I am afraid the master is not in.'

Later in the day, the 'lord of the manor' and his side were in the field and he added to his misery by putting down a couple of easy catches at slip. Well aware of some muttering in the deep, and not wanting to lose face by moving himself from his appointed position, he called across to his butler: 'I'm having some difficulty with sighting the ball in this light. Kindly hold up the game and fetch my spectacles.' Although the afternoon was bright and sunny, the butler duly obliged, returning a few moments later. The spectacles did not work the hoped-for miracle. Yet another straightforward edge lobbed to slip and fell through clutching fingers onto the floor. The silence was broken by the fumbling fielder. 'Damn it all, Carruthers, you fool, you've brought out my reading spectacles,' he complained.

Frank Chester, one of the umpires who rightly earned a reputation for getting it right nearly all the time, liked a flutter on the horses and, in company with so many cricketers with a matching interest, had to spend some anxious hours out in the middle wondering what had happened in the 2.30 or 3.00 race at York or Newmarket. In 1924 at Taunton he had discussed racing with some of the Somerset team and told them of a decent wager he had placed. In the middle of the afternoon a wicket fell and Somerset's regular last man emerged from the pavilion, having been promoted in the order.

From his first ball he called for an impossible single and was run out by a comfortable distance. Chester had no option but to give the decision against him. 'Don't worry about that, Frank,' said the batsman cheerfully as he marched away. 'I only came out to tell you that your horse has won and that the lads are expecting a few pints all round at the close.'

Local rivalry between neighbouring sides can be razor-edged. The annual match is just as important to them as any Test, more so, in fact, for they have to live with the consequences of the result for a year, suffering good-natured ribbing if they lose, while being able to boast continually over twelve months about their prowess if they win. In a particular game one side had recruited a 'ringer' – a good club cricketer accustomed to operating at a much higher level – who happened to be courting one of the village girls.

Never one to look a gift horse in the mouth, the captain persuaded him to turn out for the derby contest and he duly opened the innings. Immediately he set about the rustic bowling with a wide range of handsome attacking strokes, but as the runs flowed he made the fundamental error of allowing a loose delivery to hit him on the leg as he moved down the pitch. His experience told him it was a matter of no consequence, he could not be out. 'Howzat!' appealed the youthful bowler, more in hope than anything. 'That's out,' confirmed the ancient umpire. The star batsman gave a look of surprise before setting off for the pavilion. 'I thought I walked a long way forward to that one, umpire,' he suggested. 'Aye, no doubt you did, but not as far as I would have had to walk if I'd given you not out. The bowler delivers the papers and t' shop's over a mile from my house.'

The batsman's potential for enjoyment is always limited by an outside influence and it is definitely annoying to be given out by mistake. He might have waited all week for his one innings on a Saturday afternoon, spent a couple of nights in the nets practising, and upset his wife by refusing to go shopping, only to be sent packing lbw to a ball that pitched a foot outside leg stump. Once the umpire's finger goes up, that's it. All that might be left is a bit of leather-hunting in the field. It's not like soccer, where players have the scope to be involved for the whole ninety minutes.

Cricket, of course, is a very social game and one of the many delights for the club player is the holiday tour. These can be either very serious men-only affairs, with every day taken up with sport, or the more gentle variety which allow for the presence of wives and girlfriends.

A good opening batsman, who had made plenty of runs with his university side, joined a group for a casual visit to the Home Counties. It was a mixed trip, with only four fixtures and plenty of time for sight-seeing, so his young lady, who had led rather a sheltered life, took the chance of taking a look at something of the world – or at least London – by accompanying him.

Sadly, he had a miserable run, being very much out of touch, and, to his great annoyance in the final match, when he at last got to grips with his timing, he fell victim to a dreadful lbw decision from an umpire whose interest in the events appeared to be no more than passing.

Controlling himself with a great act of will-power, the young batsman matched off in silence. But his holiday had been ruined. The next day he took his young lady around the big city, with which he was quite familiar, pointing out such sights as Oxford Street, the Duke of Wellington's old home, Hyde Park, Marble Arch and all the other places with names that capture the imagination. Eventually in Trafalgar Square, while his companion was feeding the pigeons, he was approached by another young lady, this time of distinctly doubtful virtue. He quickly walked on, but his girlfriend became persistent in her enquiries as to what had taken place, the more so as she initially thought he must have known the other female.

As all men are aware, when a woman wants to know something there is no point in trying to dodge the issue, so eventually our hero had to explain. Having lived in a quiet rural area all her life, his girlfriend was genuinely shocked. She spent some minutes considering all the angles and then asked: 'But what happens if they have a baby?' 'Oh, that's easy,' he replied. 'They turn into umpires when they grow up.'

Unquestionably W. G. Grace, the greatest of all crick-eters in the opinion of the majority, has become associated with most stories about batsmen challenging the umpire's authority. Most of them, I am sure, are either complete invention or have been embellished with the telling. It is probable, however, that Grace did argue the point out in the middle and it is reasonable to accept that more often than not he was right.

The standards of umpiring today are very high. I know there have been incidents and disputes in some Test matches, but overall the position is more than acceptable. When Grace played, many umpires were rough and ready men who knew far less about the game than he did, so it might be argued that he taught many of them important lessons in the best sense of the word.

I don't believe the story of Grace, having been bowled, putting the bails back on and suggesting: 'A bit windy today.' The umpire is supposed to have replied: 'Yes, mind it doesn't blow off your cap on the way back to the pavilion.' That, to my mind, is part of the inevitable fiction that attaches itself to the really great in any walk of life. Geoff Boycott is another to become the centre of flights of fancy, while Fred Trueman has been known, with 'absolute certainty' to be in something like twenty different public houses in one town at the same time.

Still, many of the anecdotes about Grace reflect the public view and they may also contain more than a hint of his character. Some are demonstrably true, and I always chuckle at the report of a meeting between Grace and one of the many dour Yorkshiremen who crossed his path.

Joe Rowbotham, born in Sheffield near the Bramall Lane ground, was a typical product of the area – solid and reliable with an unshakeable faith in his own ability and a streak of determination running right through him. When he retired as a batsman, he became an umpire and stood in a match at Nottingham which involved Grace. He gave him out caught at the wicket. 'Joe, what have you done?' asked the champion, rubbing his arm in an attempt to convince Rowbotham that the ball had struck him there. 'Given you out, doctor,' came the reply. 'And I shall do it again if it happens. That one came off your glove.' Rowbotham had played long enough himself and needed no instruction on the finer points.

A less assured man might have given Grace the benefit of the doubt. Certainly there were indications that he had been slightly favoured once against Essex, for whom Charles Kortwright, an amateur fast bowler, was in full cry. Among his contemporaries, Kortwright was regarded as the fastest bowler who had ever lived and, by all accounts, he had a temperament to match his pace. A number of passionate appeals for lbw and catches behind the wicket were rejected as Grace continued his innings until a terrific yorker wrecked his wicket. The doctor could not argue with that, so he departed, Kortwright followed him to say: 'Surely you are not going? There's one stump still standing.'

Another celebrated comment associated with Grace came from a high-born man behind the stumps, Lord Cobham, and is therefore utterly reliable. I have been convinced for many years that umpires and wicketkeepers make very good selectors. They, after all, see more than anyone else and are at the heart of the action. Thus a good man behind the stumps fills two roles – firstly in his

'Surely you are not going? There's one stump still standing.'

capacity as a specialist and secondly as an advisor to his captain. Jimmy Binks, for example, did much more than simply keep wicket in a very fine Yorkshire side in the 1960s. Jimmy offered a stream of useful suggestions to his skipper Brian Close, who could also rely on the expertise of Ray Illingworth. No wonder Yorkshire took some beating.

As an aside, Chris Balderstone, now an umpire after playing for Yorkshire, Leicestershire and England, has clear memories of his early experience of joining his native county's first team. Yorkshire were in the field and a wicket had fallen. Chris quietly joined the general gathering around the stumps at the batsman's end and listened to the hum of conversation. All eyes were fixed on the dressing room and as the next man appeared the plans were laid. Between them the congregation of hard-headed Yorkshiremen had a very good idea of what he could and could not do. 'From where I stood, it seemed impossible for the newcomer to make a single run,' said Chris, 'And I should not have been surprised if they had known what he had for breakfast as well as his inside leg measurement.'

Binks would have noted as a matter of course any strengths and weaknesses among all the opposition ranks. Similarly Lord Cobham was able to make a sound assessment of Grace. 'He had all the strokes and all the time he required to play them to the fullest effect,' he said, adding, almost as an after-thought: 'He also had the dirtiest neck I ever kept wicket behind.'

As a general rule, of course, it is customary to give the batsman the benefit of the doubt. Not all of us are as convinced of our infallibility as Frank Chester. 'When I give a decision, there is no doubt,' he said. But in reality there has to be some, notably in close run-out situations.

Alec Skelding put the umpire's dilemma neatly into perspective. In dealing with what the Duke of Wellington might have referred to as a 'near-run thing', Alec shook his head ruefully at the hopeful fieldsman. 'It's really a photo-finish,' he ruled, 'But as we don't have a camera handy, not out.'

There are, though, exceptions to any rule and the genial Schofield Haigh provided one. Had it not been for Wilfred Rhodes and George Hirst, with whom he played regularly, Haigh might well have been regarded as the greatest all-rounder to grace the Yorkshire ranks. A brilliant cricketer, he also had a marvellous sense of fun, enjoying every minute of his life whether winning or losing. He, too, joined the ranks of the umpires and during a Scarborough Festival encounter gave out Yorkshire's John Tunnicliffe to a dubious catch at the wicket. The batsman, not too pleased with the outcome, decided to debate the issue during an interval. 'Were you really sure I got an edge?' he asked. 'No, not really,' replied Haigh. 'Then why did you give me out?' 'Well, while making up my mind, I noticed the expression on your face and thought you looked very guilty.'

This, all joking apart, is a serious element. I have known many batsmen who will do anything to distract the umpire if they think they might be lbw, calling their partner for a leg-bye for instance, while making sure they move their legs. When they think they are reasonably safe, on the other hand, they remain stationary, with their leg at the point of impact, indicating, in their mind, the folly of the appeal.

These antics are something that umpires get used to as they attempt a balanced judgment, shutting out everything except what they have seen. Another little trick adopted by some batsmen is to turn their back on the umpire. I am not sure what they expect to gain unless they feel that the official will be reluctant to raise his finger and stand there with no one taking much notice. I must say that one famous England player got into this habit, but Fred Jakeman upstaged him.

Fred made a lot of runs for Northamptonshire after

moving down from Yorkshire and then gained a place on the first class umpires' list. Quite quickly he decided that when giving a decision in favour of the bowler he would also call loudly: 'That's out.' Eventually, he came across the famous England opener out in the middle. 'Tell me, Fred, why do you always shout when you give anyone out?' he was asked. 'To let buggers like you know to get on your way,' Fred said.

Overall, however, it has to be said that there is a very good relationship between the umpires and players, especially on the English circuit, where we can have a drink and a chat afterwards. People often think that fast bowlers such as Dennis Lillee and Jeff Thomson were difficult to control. Nothing could be further from the truth. I can honestly say they were good competitors, but also accepted decisions with good grace. Even so, they liked a bit of leg-pulling along the way. When I first came into contact with Dennis, I turned down what he obviously felt was a good lbw shout. 'Crikey, you must be blind,' he muttered as he walked back to his mark. 'What's that?' I enquired, cupping a hand to my ear. 'Oh God, deaf as well,' he added with a big grin.

It is, incidentally, surprising how some of the most battle-hardened old professionals react. Norman Gifford simply went on and on as a slow left-arm bowler, moving from Worcestershire to Warwickshire, but all along he retained his drive and he never liked to lose. He gave nothing away and rarely failed to air his views. I umpired with Kevin Lyons, the former Glamorgan wicketkeeper, at Hove in 1985 when Sussex met Warwickshire and piled up the runs on a featherbed pitch.

They scored 405 for three in the first innings and 228 for two in the second and, while Warwickshire replied solidly enough to secure a draw, this did nothing to mollify Norman. He got through thirty overs for ninety runs on the first day and had not been that close to success when

Gehan Mendis padded a ball away, provoking a passionate appeal to Kevin for an lbw decision. 'Not out,' said Kevin. 'You must be joking,' roared Norman. 'Still not out,' confirmed Kevin. Norman stalked across the pitch to where I was standing at square leg. 'What do you think to that, Dickie?' he asked. 'Don't be silly, Norman, it's nothing to do with me,' I told him. 'Well, I'd still like a second opinion,' he snorted as he stomped back to his mark, kicking a few imaginary tufts of grass on the way.

Arguably the most difficult law for the umpires to enforce is the one relating to throwing. This is, of course, a controversial subject, provoking many arguments down the years and one or two unpleasant scenes as well. I always feel that it is impossible for a bowler who really tweaks it to have a ramrod-straight arm, and I know that Ian Peebles, the England and Middlesex leg-spinner and much admired writer on cricket, spent a lot of time studying bowling actions. He came to the conclusion that spinners could not flight the ball without some straightening of the arm.

Umpires know only too well that if they call someone for throwing – or, to be more accurate in modern terms, merely report his action – they might be taking a step that will lead to the end of a career. No one likes the thought of this possibility, but we have to uphold the laws.

Tony Lock, one of the most aggressive of all cricketers, who bowled his left-arm stuff as if his life depended on the outcome, was under suspicion, to say the least, for a lengthy spell before getting into serious trouble. He dismissed Doug Insole when bowling for Surrey against the Rest at the Oval in 1955, but the batsman momentarily stood his ground. 'That's out,' snarled Tony. 'I know that,' admitted Insole. 'I just wondered whether I had been bowled or run out.'

Another bowler with quite a reputation caused an umpire concern. The official, being both conscientious and kind-hearted, decided to have a quiet word with his captain at lunch. 'I have to say I think he throws,' the umpire confided. 'Oh, yes,''admitted the captain. 'But he throws them so quick and straight that we have kept him in the side.'

I suppose it would be impossible to write about umpires without mentioning the light. This is the one thing that upsets the public more than anything. Sadly, in trying to be fair to both sides, umpires in general and yours truly in particular seem to become the villains of the piece. This is neither the time nor place to go into a long debate about bad light, but I would just say that I have consistently advocated playing through all light unless the umpire is convinced there is a genuine physical danger to the batsman.

Allan Border, the Australian captain, is one influential figure who agrees and, as he points out, it is normally to the advantage of one side or the other to go off.

A couple of situations spring to mind. During a match at Old Trafford a Lancashire member accosted me as we left the field. He was not threatening, but he had been having the odd drink and he wanted to make his point. 'What's up now Birdie?' he asked. 'Tha aren't bringing 'em off again for bad leet, are' tha'?' 'Certainly not, sir,' I was able to inform him. 'I am happy to say that the conditions are perfect, but this is the luncheon interval which we are taking strictly according to the regulations covering championship matches.' That shook him.

Just as an aside on a similar theme, I heard of a pushy young broadcaster called in at the last minute to do some cricket for a local radio station. The regular reporter had been taken ill at the last minute and his replacement had established a reputation for being a lively Jack-of-all-Trades rather than an expert on any one thing.

Nevertheless, he assured the producer he knew all there was to know about cricket and set out on the assignment.

This involved providing up-to-date scores at given times and then adding a bit of commentary into the running sports programme as required.

Everything went fine. He gave the scores all right and handled the first bit of commentary without dropping any clangers. Suddenly, however, he became very excited. 'Wait a minute, there's something going on here. Some of the fielders are walking off. The rest are following. Now the batsmen are setting off for the pavilion as well. The umpires have taken off the bails. It must be some sort of protest.' Finally his rising voice was cut off, just as someone whispered in the background. 'For heaven's sake, Steve, it's the tea interval.'

I inadvertently caused a few hearts to miss a beat during the Oval Test between England and New Zealand in 1986. I learned later that there was a good deal of concern among the customers when I walked across to my partner, David Shepherd. Dark threatening clouds had been building up for some time and it had become a bit on the gloomy side. An agonised cry rose from someone in the packed ranks of spectators. 'Nay, Dickie, don't take them off again.' David and I exchanged a few smiles. I merely wanted the new ball which he had been keeping, but we got a round of applause when the action continued.

So to my most embarrassing moment. A two-hour session can be a long time when you suddenly discover that you want to go to the toilet. It is fairly easy for the players. They can nip off for a couple of minutes without anyone noticing, but the poor old umpire is, as they say, centre stage. For him, the show never stops. As a consequence, it is important to have your body well trained and it is very rare for me to have problems.

During the 1984 Old Trafford Test between England and West Indies, however, I realised that I must go to the bathroom with well over an hour before the next break. Gordon Greenidge and Jeff Dujon were batting, with Ian

'It must be some sort of protest.'

Botham bowling. Ian, in fact, had a rather wayward spell, for which I might have been partly – if innocently – to blame. I told him of my predicament. 'Shall I dig you a little hole?' he enquired, making a scraping motion with his foot. 'No, thank you, but you can hold the fort while I run off,' I replied. That was the only thing I could do and the spectators gave me a tremendous ovation when I returned. On regaining my position I said: 'Gentlemen, for this relief much thanks,' and we got things under way again.

||| 4 |||

No Laughing Matter

Cricket has always been too important to Yorkshiremen to be played just for fun. In an area where life has usually been pretty hard in terms of earning a living, time away from work was too precious to be wasted on mere frivolity. It still is. This is why we play the game differently. I have lived all my life in Barnsley, which is typical of much of the county, and from the toddlers upwards everything is pursued with a real competitive enthusiasm.

Kids playing in the street have to organise some sort of competition, and not many subscribe to the Olympic ideal that competing is the important thing. Winning is what matters to Yorkshiremen, especially at cricket.

Thus very few find anything wrong with the principle of the bowler running out any batsman who strays out of his ground at the moment of delivery. To the average league player the batsman is simply stealing an unfair advantage, so he is fair game. In the circumstances, umpires really have to have their heart in their business, for they do a thankless job and have to keep their wits about them all the time. At the end of the day they get very little financial reward, but they can expect at best a pretty keen argument from somebody or other who feels they have received a bad decision. That's life, as they say, and sport would not survive without thousands of dedicated officials who give far more than they ever receive.

Even then, I don't suppose for a minute that they are

half as worried about the job as some more famous officials I have come across all over the world. It's no use going out into the middle in some countries with a faint heart. One village umpire in a faraway place once told me: 'It's not just getting your decision right. You mustn't upset the spectators or you could get home and find your house on fire!'

I'm not sure to this day whether he was telling the truth, but I saw him in action and the crowd were certainly doing a lot of shouting. India is a good example. My old friend Swarup Krishnan has a very big reputation out there – nearly as big as his huge frame. We must have looked like Laurel and Hardy when we operated together in the Asia Cup in Sharjah in 1984. More than one spinner has said to me: 'It's like bowling round a traffic island.'

I remember Swarup telling me about the problems he and his colleagues had to face. 'Dickie,' he said, 'our spectators get so carried away by the game. When England are batting in a Test at Bombay, there are 50,000 Indians wanting a wicket with every ball and appealing whenever a batsman is hit on the legs. It's worse in Calcutta. There are 90,000 there letting you know what they think. I tell you, it's important to concentrate all the time to save your skin.'

That's another story, though. Back to Yorkshire. There are a lot of stories about wicketkeepers, some of whom have been real villains. A local league batsman recently suggested at a cricket dinner: 'The only difference between most wicketkeepers and Dick Turpin is that Turpin had the decency to wear a mask.'

An old trick used to be to stick a hairgrip in the front of the right boot so that the offstump could be nudged if the ball passed close to it, although the wicketkeeper had to be good enough to stand up, of course. An experienced rogue could add to the confusion by waving his gloves about and shouting 'Well bowled!' But it has to be said

'It's like bowling round a traffic island.'

that this is marked as unfair cheating.

Wicketkeepers have every chance of becoming characters and, like goalkeepers at soccer, they have to be a bit mad at times. One local league hero of my experience became well known throughout the area for giving the bowlers a 'bit of help'. From time to time, of course, he got involved in pretty fierce arguments, but I remember him telling me: 'I'd rather get a batsman out by outsmarting him than by taking an easy catch. There's more fun in a bit of mischief.' That, though, I thought, was taking gamesmanship too far.

A more acceptable bit of skulduggery involves the fieldsman pretending to lose the ball. Many local games are played in pretty rough fields, with buttercups, daisies and patches of long grass. I have even known 'special rules' be brought in when a farmer has had his cows in the field. Usually these meant having to roll the ball back along the ground to the bowler or wicketkeeper!

It was pretty easy in some cases for an older hand to kid a green youngster by looking around anxiously when the ball went in his direction, calling out something like: 'Where's it gone? Come and help me find the thing or they'll run hundreds.' Unwary batsmen have been persuaded to rush down the pitch, only to find themselves stranded by the sudden appearance of the ball and a straight throw.

Sleight of hand is also practised on the first-class grounds and I have never seen anybody quicker than Phil Sharpe, the old Yorkshire, Derbyshire and England batsman who became a Test selector. 'Sharpy' could catch pigeons at slip, as they say, and when in an impish mood he would slip the ball into his pocket like lightning and turn with everyone else to look in the direction of the third-man boundary. After a suitable interval, he would pull the ball out of his pocket with a quiet smile. The late

Johnny Wardle could also do the odd conjuring trick, which reminds me of one of cricket's longest-lived and most popular characters, Jack Mercer.

Dear old Jack, the Northamptonshire scorer for many years, was ninety-two when he died in 1987 after giving so much to the game. I got to know him very well because it is usual for the umpires to have their luncheon with the 'chalkers' at county games and, since we are in contact all day through signalling to each other, a natural bond develops. Jack could do the sort of tricks that give magicians a good living on television and he did them right there in front of you, pulling all manner of objects out of your ear or nose. Nobody played cards with him.

He served as an officer in the Russian cavalry in 1914 before becoming a very effective bowler with Sussex, Glamorgan and Northamptonshire. His record included ten for 51 in one innings for Glamorgan against Worcestershire at Worcester in 1936, and I used to ask him if that had been a conjuring trick too. Jack had a storehouse full of stories, and the one he enjoyed best concerned an attempt to get rid of the great Jack Hobbs cheaply.

Like all county sides, Glamorgan did not like having to face Surrey and their high-scoring opener, who ranks up there with Don Bradman among the best batsmen of all time. This particular year, however, they came up with a plan. Jack, a great student of tactics, had noticed over the years that Hobbs tended to get off the mark straight away, often just pushing the ball to cover's left hand to collect an easy single. 'It was probably just a little mannerism, but I thought we could turn it to our advantage,' Jack said.

Glamorgan happened to have a left-handed fielder in their side that season. This sometimes happens. Yorkshire's Phil Robinson is a right-handed batsman, but he throws in with his left and he surprised one or two batsmen in his first couple of seasons. As they approached the Surrey game, the Glamorgan lads put in a bit of secret practice. Jack bowled, the batsman pushed the ball out on the offside and set out for a run. The left-handed cover pounced and hurled the ball to the bowler's end, where mid-on had hurried into position over the top of the stumps.

It worked like a charm. After a week Glamorgan were running out the batsman by half the length of the pitch, so they arrived for the Surrey match quietly confident. No matter how often he told it, Jack always enjoyed the punch line. 'I knew I had to bowl one just short of a length around the off stump,' he said. 'But when the big day came, I was so keen to put the ball where Hobbs could push it for one that I gave him a big half-volley. He smashed it for four and got a hundred!'

A naturally generous man, Jack was always ready to lend a helping hand to anyone in trouble. An opponent had the misfortune to pick the Glamorgan fixture for his benefit match and it had been badly hit by rain. In the past, a benefit was a one-off occasion and not the twelve-month affair that has become the modern norm. The unhappy cricketer had taken the sensible precaution of taking out insurance, but that came into effect only if there was no play at all.

Sadly an improvement in the weather came too late to persuade any spectators to pay their entrance money, so when the umpires began to consider the possibility of a start after tea the beneficiary looked likely to be out of pocket all round. The ground had no more than basic covers for the wicket, with guttering around the edges which gathered the water into four buckets, one being posted at each corner.

Jack, as an experienced professional, got permission to go out with his captain when the umpires made an inspection. Clumsily, he stumbled when he reached the middle, 'accidentally' kicking over one of the buckets which spilled its contents over the pitch.

'Oh well,' he apologised, 'it's an ill wind that blows nobody any good. At least, the insurance money will come in handy to buy me a pint when we've called play off for the day.'

Now and again, of course, things can go wrong because of something outside the control of the fielding side. Essex, under the dashing leadership of Brian 'Tonker' Taylor, were never short of ideas and in one of their inventive moods they set out to trick a well-known compulsive hooker. In the course of an over, square leg moved a little farther back. The fourth ball was the bouncer, and as it was on its way down the wicket the fieldsman set off running towards the boundary. Sure enough, the batsman hooked it high and hard and would have lost his wicket to a brilliant catch – had not the umpire called 'no ball'. The bowler found himself the target of some harsh words until the official explained that he had not no-balled him for overstepping. 'It's your fault, skipper,' he told Taylor, 'You've three men behind square leg.' The laws, of course, allow only two. Some quick counting went on before the penny dropped. 'I hope you aren't counting the chap right on the boundary edge,' said Taylor. 'Of course I am,' replied the umpire. 'That's not a fielder, it's the ruddy ice cream man,' roared the luckless Essex captain.

Things can sometimes work the other way, too. It is common practice to allow the batsman a single off the mark from the first ball in his benefit match. This is a polite tradition which is widely appreciated, but I recall standing in a county match when things went badly wrong. The beneficiary acknowledged the expected applause as he marched out to the wicket, took his guard and confidently went onto the front foot to pick up his run from the expected gentle half-volley. Halfway through his strike, however, he realised that the young fast bowler at the

'That's not a fielder, it's the ruddy ice cream man.'

other end was not fulfilling his part of the bargain. A nasty
lifter took the shoulder of a hastily raised defensive bat
and the ball lobbed into the gulley, where a slightly embar-
rassed opponent took the catch.

'What the heck were you doing?' asked the captain after
apologising to the disgruntled batsman. 'Well,' replied the
bowler, 'you said "let him have one," so I did.' I imagine
he soon realised he had misunderstood the message.

Mark you, I have always thought that the spoken word
can lead to confusion, and my friends among the journalists who write about cricket agree. I have mentioned before
a mistake by Robin Marlar, the old Sussex captain who
became an influential commentator on the game with the
Sunday Times. That incident involved the West Indian
pace attack at Old Trafford in 1976, when England's
opening pair of John Edrich and Brian Close found themselves ducking and weaving under a barrage of bouncers.
Marlar wrote: 'Bird stood like a pillar at square leg and
did nothing about it.'

The reason I took no action was that I happened to be
officiating in a championship game in the South. Lloyd
Budd was, in fact, the umpire concerned, but, as Robin
explained, the difference between Bird and Budd to a
copytaker 200 miles away is very small and whoever took
down the report simply misheard. There have been literally thousands of other instances and another of my
favourite cricketing people, Big Bill Bowes, was the victim
when he worked for the *Yorkshire Evening Post*. After he
retired from active service, Bill, one of the best bowlers
Yorkshire and England ever had, covered cricket on a
day-by-day basis, telephoning his reports to the office.

In a report from the Scarborough Festival Bill said:
'After a quiet spell, Parfitt went down the wicket to Illingworth and edged him over the slips and into the deep for
￢ee.' That, however, came out rather differently at the
￢ther end. A girl who had no interest in cricket typed it

74

down as: 'After a quiet spell, Parfitt went down the wicket to Illingworth and edged him over the cliffs and into the deepest part of the sea.'

Now I know Scarborough is a seaside town, but that is ridiculous. There are plenty of equally strange examples of the same thing. When Bob White, who is now on the first class umpires' list, was still playing with Nottinghamshire there was an amusing misprint in a local paper. Bad light had stopped play, but in transmission this turned into 'Bob White stops play'. Another time 'two damp spots on the pitch' became 'two lamp-posts on the pitch', while 'the batsmen really enjoyed a series of full tosses' was translated into 'the batsmen really enjoyed a series of full coffees'.

Reporters also insist that all newspaper offices are inhabited by a strange creature called a printer's devil which pops up when no-one is looking to slip the odd misprint into the columns. When Reg Simpson earned his first England cap in the late 1940s, his local Nottingham evening paper rightly made a big story out of his arrival on the international scene. They also added a lot of background material, including the fact that he had been in the special branch at one time. 'Simpson has been a detective in the local police farce,' they told their readers. Obviously it did not take long for the slip to be spotted, so next night the editor put in a correction. 'We apologise for an error in our story about Reg Simpson in yesterday's edition,' it said. 'The sentence should have read: "Simpson has been a defective in the local police force."' I gather they gave it up after that. Reg, one of the very best post-war batsmen, particularly against hostile fast bowling, took it all in good part.

Bill Bowes enjoyed – if that is the word – another adventure at Bradford. The pavilion has been pulled down now, but the Press Box was situated on the front at one end. It was a low, narrow room with windows that opened out onto the rows of members' seats, so when they were open in warm weather the public could hear a lot of what was going on. Yorkshire were working hard without much success against Warwickshire, who had been in the fore-front of signing overseas stars, and the game had reached a stalemate.

Bill's regular copytaker, Lillian – Lilly for short – was temporarily away from her post at the time of his call to the office. So a deputy, considerably less familiar with cricket and its terminology, stepped into the breach.

She could not understand much of what Bill was saying and constantly interrupted the flow of his copy. Gradually his normally good temper gave way under pressure as he repeated each sentence several times. Finally a very loud voice he roared: 'Oh, for heavens' sake put Lilly on.' At this someone from the members' area shouted: 'Crikey! Don't tell me they've signed him an' all.'

Mention of Scarborough reminds me of another mis-understanding, this time from the dark and distant past. The North Marine Road ground is one of the most pleasant in the country and there is always a good atmosphere created by the enthusiastic holiday crowds. One of the great men associated with Scarborough and the famous Festival was Charles Inglis Thornton, better known as 'Buns', who had the reputation of being a tremendously big hitter.

At the town end of the ground is Trafalgar Square and some very tall three-storey houses back onto the playing area. In 1886, playing for The Gentlemen against I Zingari, Thornton hit a ball from A. G. Steel, a well-known Test cricketer of that era, over the houses. I am told he actually cleared the third chimney to the onside of a gap in the row of houses, so those of you who visit Scarborough can see for yourselves what a massive blow it must have been.

Only one other man, that Australian ace Cec Pepper, who became a colourful umpire, has equalled that effort –

in 1945 – although Yorkshire's scorer Ted Lester, who is a Scarborian and played many innings there in both club and county cricket, tried hard to do it throughout his career. But back to Thornton. Word of his feat naturally spread and a few weeks later at a social gathering in London a lady came up to him and politely asked: 'Tell me, Mr Thornton, were you batting at Lord's or the Oval when you hit the ball into Trafalgar Square?'

Big hitting, of course, usually sparks off the humorists, for there is something about the helpless frustration of the bowler which has a similar appeal to that of a man slipping on a banana skin.

Arthur Wood, one of Yorkshire's great line of brilliant wicketkeepers, once made even the normally reserved Hedley Verity smile when he must have felt like crying. The scene yet again was Bradford's Park Avenue ground, one of the smaller venues on the first-class circuit, with the stand of the Football League club invitingly handy for the straight drive. Kent's Frank Woolley, never a man to miss an opportunity, was enjoying himself at Verity's expense bombarding the roof with a barrage of sweetly-timed sixes.

Wood called himself 'Rhubarb' because in a strong Yorkshire batting side he reckoned he always had to go in to 'force' the pace, and he invariably saw the funny side of everything. 'Eeh, it's fair grand just now, Hedley,' he said to the anguished bowler as they changed ends after another expensive over. 'How do you make that out?' asked Verity. 'Why, with the ball going rat-a-tat-tat, rat-a-tat-tat on the roof of the stand, it's like having a boy scout band playing in the background,' replied Wood.

Bradford was also the setting for a vigorous assault on Yorkshire slow left armer Phil Carrick by John Inchmore, the Worcestershire pace bowler. Although regularly among the late-order batsman, Inchmore could hit very well once he had got his eye in, and after a lean time in

'Tell me, Mr Thornton, were you batting at Lord's or The Oval
when you hit the ball into Trafalgar Square?'

the field he had every incentive to get a bit of his own back when the sides clashed at Park Avenue in 1980.

Yorkshire, having scored 334 in their first innings, had visions of a nice lead when they captured the sixth Worcestershire wicket at 241. Inchmore, however, found Carrick very much to his liking as he smashed seven sixes in the course of a blistering half-century. While he peppered the football ground, Yorkshire's acting captain Richard Lumb wore an increasingly puzzled frown, finding it hard to decide whether to replace Carrick, who might easily get the wicket any ball as Inchmore slogged away.

Noticing his dilemma, the ever-present wag in the crowd stepped in with some unwelcome advice. 'Leave him on, Richard,' he called. 'Inchmore's all right on the reds, but he could have difficulty when he gets on to the colours.'

Without doubt Jack Simmons is one of the most popular characters to have graced county cricket. He is a big, easy-going, good-natured chap with a refreshing attitude, although he is also a very competitive professional and does not miss many tricks. He is, of course, best known as Flat Jack, a name which reflects the 'mean' nature of his slow bowling. He does not give the ball much air, but pushes it through at the batsman.

Jack told me that his style was the result of playing on soft wickets as a youngster, and it was Tony Nicholson, the Yorkshire bowler with a ready wit, who gave Jack his nickname. We'll come to Tony again later, but he helped out as a television commentator when Yorkshire met Lancashire in a special match at Tewkesbury, in Gloucestershire, to celebrate the Wars of the Roses. As Simmons came on to bowl, Tony just said: 'Here comes Flat Jack,' and the name has stuck.

As a matter of fact, Jack displayed more than just a bit of promise as a soccer player with his home town club of Great Harwood. He insists he was a fearless bustling centre-forward with the knack of knocking in the goals, and I, for one, believe him. Everton were once interested in putting him on their books, but nothing came of it in the end. It's funny, by the way, how many good cricketers might have made a living at the winter game. That's another subject that will crop up later, but it's worth noting that Bill Athey, the Gloucestershire and England batsman, attracted a lot of attention before he joined Yorkshire and Geoff Boycott impressed Leeds United scouts at an early age.

Probably Jack took the fact that he broke a leg three times in ten months as a sign that life in football was not for him, and Lancashire must be eternally grateful. His calm presence at times of crisis has made the difference between victory and defeat so often.

He also has a good appetite and if he ever goes sight-seeing it's usually around the butchers' shops – or so his team-mates say. He rightly enjoyed a record benefit of £128,000 for Lancashire in 1980 and, as a result, became known in some quarters as the shy millionaire. In the 1987 season I officiated in a Lancashire match and noticed that Jack, fielding at mid-on and mid-off, was not bending to stop the ball. If it came near enough he shoved out a boot to stop it and then kicked it to someone else.

'What's all this about, have you gone on strike?' I asked between overs. 'I'm a bit stiff today,' he admitted. 'The back's playing me up a bit.' 'You'll have to call it a day and retire then,' I joked. 'Oh, no,' he exclaimed. 'I'm hoping to play on for another benefit.'

It was in the same game that I lost my voice. Lancashire's West Indian fast bowler, Pat Patterson, had some difficulty with his front foot and I had to call him a few times for overstepping. The strain must have been too much, for on the fifth or sixth occasion I discovered I could hardly raise a whisper. 'For goodness sake, don't bowl any more no-balls,' I croaked. 'It's all right,' the player agreed. 'You can carry on using sign language.' Happily a quick gargle during the interval helped and Pat got his rhythm back, so I got through the day without too much difficulty.

||| 5 |||

A Few Bouncers

I have never really thought cricket to be a dangerous game, but it isn't exactly safe, either, and you need guts as well as ability to play at almost any level. Indeed, on some of the rough, under-prepared strips in club cricket it may well help if you are slightly mad. Winston Churchill summed up the outsider's view when he told Colin Cowdrey: 'I only played when I was a small boy at school, and the one memory I have is that the ball was very hard.'

That is definitely true and I have taken some nasty knocks as an umpire. A truly painful one came at Chesterfield in 1983, when Ken McEwan of Essex pulled a long hop from Derbyshire's left-arm spinner Dallas Moir straight onto my shin bone and I had to be carried off. Then, in the 1986 Test series between England and Australia, Graham Gooch hammered a delivery from leg-spinner Bob Holland straight back down the track. With no opportunity to get out of the way, I again took the full force, this time on my ankle. Down I went, and while I rolled about in pain I heard Gooch moaning that he had been restricted to just a single for a shot well worth a boundary. 'Never mind, sport,' said Holland. 'I think you're fair dinkum, Dickie, you saved me three runs.'

Those injuries were, of course, the result of pure accidents. But that was definitely not the case at Old Trafford in 1987 when Salim Malik caused me a lot of pain. Tim Robinson pushed the ball to mid-wicket and we all relaxed as there was no possibility of a run. Salim Malik, however,

I have taken some nasty knocks as the umpire.

picked it up and hurled it at the non-striker's end, hitting bull's eye just below my knee. 'What are you doing? Nobody's running,' I howled. 'I know that, Dickie, I was aiming at you. Now you have something to remember me by,' he said with a big grin. He's right as well. I carry a lump on my leg to this day.

There are also quite a few bones chipped in the field, especially in the slips, and I heard of more than one Lancashire League amateur who found life in the close-catching cordon far from easy when the imported West Indian fast bowlers were letting rip. When speaking at a dinner over on the 'wrong side of the Pennines', I got into conversation with an old chap whose hands looked as if they had been trampled on by a horse. 'I made a terrible mistake,' he explained. 'We signed Learie Constantine and I took a couple of good catches at slip in his first game. He kept me there for the rest of the season and I've had rheumatism ever since.'

Mostly, however, the batsmen get the worst of it and even in these days of highly sophisticated protection there is plenty of exposed flesh to be hurt. Geoff Boycott took a lot of care in preparing for his lengthy visits to the wicket, using tape, padding and protection. 'Watching you pad up, Fiery, is like seeing an instalment of *Emergency Ward 10*,' Graham Stevenson observed in the Yorkshire dressing room.

Fred Trueman, of course, figures prominently in accounts of misadventure and Peter Parfitt, who accumulated runs regularly for Middlesex and England, recalls his first encounter with him. The match was at Lord's and Fred had somehow heard that Peter rather fancied himself as a good hooker of the short ball. 'Tha'll get a bit o' practice today, sunshine,' Fred promised and, sure enough, Parfitt's arrival prompted a barrage of hostile short-pitched stuff. He took an immediate blow in that most sensitive of areas – 'one in 't box to start wi', exclaimed Fred – and finally Peter gloved one into his face, retiring to have the wound dressed.

Although feeling distinctly groggy, Parfitt did not want to give any impression of fear and when it was suggested he could resume at the fall of the next wicket he agreed, albeit reluctantly. As he made his way back to the middle, encouraged by the ripple of sympathetic applause, he was greeted by the mildly impressed Trueman, who observed: 'Tha's got something, sunshine, they don't usually come back when I've felled 'em.'

It is not always necessary for the bowling to be exceptionally quick for the batsmen to be afraid for their lives. Rain-affected pitches have caused havoc in the past and I have seen some strange conditions affect play. I remember one freak incident at Buxton in June 1975, when, in the middle of one of the hottest summers on record, snow stopped play. Lancashire had made 477 for five – a record for the 100-over first innings of a championship match – before a sudden blizzard covered the pitch to a good depth. It did not last long, but it left a legacy of trouble and torment for the Derbyshire batsmen. I have never experienced anything worse, for a good-length ball reared head high and Derbyshire were shot out twice for 42 and 87. But they were not too bothered about the score so long as they escaped with their limbs intact. Ashley Harvey-Walker handed me his teeth wrapped in a handkerchief when he came out. 'Look after these. I won't be long,' he said. He was right, too. He soon fell to a catch around the corner. 'Is that out?' he asked, anxiously looking round. 'I'm afraid so,' I replied. 'Thank goodness for that. Let's have my teeth, I'm well out of it,' he said, and hurried back to the dressing room.

Even Grace had a lot of respect for the quickies and the fact that he could handle them better than most did not lessen his regard for the best among their ranks. He appreciated that even the bravest batsmen might well be apprehensive on some of the rough and ready strips that served as pitches when he was piling up the runs. Out of kindness, therefore, he advised a raw and nervous batsman to 'get a box' to protect himself. The novice duly did as he was told, but in his day they did not enjoy the range of choice available to the modern batsman. He had to settle for a complicated contraption constructed of bent wire which, however, did the trick.

He definitely needed its protection, for he was beaten and struck about the body almost at will by the bowler and each time the ball struck his large and cumbersome box the wires twanged tunefully. The Doctor, marvelling at this development, eventually marched down the wicket, glared at his trembling partner and said in his high-pitched voice: 'Young man, when I told you to get a box, I did not mean a musical one.'

One of the great regrets of my life is that we cannot see the heroes of the past. Future generations will be able to study in detail the brilliant stroke-play of such as Barry and Viv Richards, David Gower, Sunil Gavaskar and numerous others, while the sheer power of Ian Botham is captured for ever in detailed films. His epic innings at Headingley in 1981, when England won after following on, can, for example, be relived by people who are not even born yet.

Just think how marvellous it would be to watch Victor Trumper, Jack Hobbs, Don Bradman, Wally Hammond and the like playing their momentous innings.

I mention this because if you look at some of the pictures in the old cricket books the poses of the players are so obviously unnatural. I suppose the effect was caused by the need to hold the position until the technically limited cameras had captured the shot and I remain convinced that the majority of the illustrations are misleading. One thing I have noticed, though, is that Grace appeared to stand with his left foot slightly raised and pointing down the pitch. This potentially made it a target for the well pitched-up delivery.

At some stage Wilfred Rhodes may have employed a similar stance. At any event, it transpires that he took a very painful blow on the left big toe from Harold Larwood. Off he went, hopping about and moaning with pain. Larwood, having appealed in the heat of the moment, rushed forward to apologise. 'Oh, Wilfred, I am sorry.' he said. 'I hope you are going to be all right.' The umpire, none other than Frank Chester, also showed a lot of sympathy. Eventually Rhodes came round a bit and gently put his foot on the floor, testing to see if the damaged joint would support his weight. 'Good, it looks as if you can walk well enough,' observed Chester. 'Yes, I think I can if you just give me another minute.' agreed Rhodes. 'You can have all the time you like when you get to the pavilion. But you'd better start that way now, because you're out lbw,' said Chester.

All the same, there is something about genuine fast bowling which raises the temperature on the coldest day, even on slow pitches that ought to give the batsman a distinct advantage. The sight of such as Ray Lindwall, Trueman or Lillee, each with a perfect action, racing in to release the ball in the course of the smooth cartwheel had spectators on the edge of their seats – and a few noted runmakers some way outside the line of the leg stump.

I am among the first to admire the art form of the slow bowlers, who claim their victims by subtlety, and Jim Laker, with nineteen wickets in the Manchester Test against Australia in 1956, became a national hero. The mesmeric Abdul Qadir is a living legend in Pakistan, too, where thousands of small boys have been encouraged by his success to practise their legspin, but for the most part, as Bob Willis used to say when captain of England, 'It's fast bowling that wins matches.'

The first thing that Frank Lowson did when the fixtures

came out was look to see when he was due at Chesterfield.
Frank, although operating in the shadow of the marvellous
Len Hutton, became firmly established in his own right,
opening the innings for Yorkshire and England with considerable success. But, for all his skill, he did not like
Chesterfield. 'The pitch is always green,' he claimed, 'and
Les Jackson and Cliff Gladwin leave me black and blue,
especially around the ribs. I am always glad when that
game is over.'

A lot of other players presumably checked for the Yorkshire match when Trueman was at the height of his powers,
and Fred, never one to hide his light, made the most of
the situation.

It was not uncommon for someone in the top half of the
order to become injured on the eve of a clash with Yorkshire and those who actually turned up were soon made
to feel uneasy. Fred was a very sociable man and made it
his habit to drop into the other dressing room for a bit of
a chat. This quickly became a monologue, in the course of
which each member of the opposition received advance
warning of his fate. 'Don't worry, sunshine, if you behave
yourself it's quite painless,' he would say to some open-
mouthed newcomer. In those days the whole Yorkshire
side waged incessant psychological warfare on the enemy.

Thus, when Fred actually hit a batsman – and, to be
fair, he always used the bouncer in the proper way as a
tactical weapon – he never said sorry. 'I've not noticed
any batsman apologising for hitting me for four,' he
growled when taken to task for his lack of concern at any
damage inflicted.

Another amusing tale with Fred in a starring role concerns him being on the receiving end. He was, in fact, a
useful striker of the ball and might have made a lot more
runs had he not been advised and, when necessary,
instructed to conserve his energies for bowling. This, by
the way, is an important point, and Ian Botham, who has

never been in the really fast class as a swing bowler, had to be tremendously strong to get through the huge workload that was put on his shoulders by Somerset, Worcestershire and England. It is no good a quickie making forty or fifty runs if, by doing so, he makes himself ineffective with the new ball. Before the war, poor old Bill Bowes, one of the few long-serving first-class cricketers to take more wickets than he scored runs, used to be deliberately run out as last man so that he could get on with the more important business.

That, though, is getting away from the point. Fred, on the day we are talking about, had picked up a few runs, which were much needed by Yorkshire, and he was enjoying himself when an over-ambitious stroke brought his downfall. He missed and took a blow in that sensitive area which gives rise to much ribald comment. He doubled up and fell to the floor, clutching the offended part of his body while the spectators, appreciating the irony of the situation, rocked with mirth. The fielding side gathered around the fallen champion, but most failed to conceal their amusement at the turn of events. Eventually Fred opened his eyes and gazed up at the ring of faces. 'Your turn'll come,' he snarled, 'and when it does, it'll be a stitching job.' At the end of the innings both the openers from the other team hurried to accompany him off the field, claiming loudly: 'We weren't laughing, Fred. We definitely weren't laughing.'

The young Trueman left an even greater impression on the Indians, for in 1952, his first summer of Test cricket, he destroyed their batting with speeds they had not previously encountered. The Headingley scoreboard read four wickets for no runs in the visitors' second innings as they hopped frantically about and took unashamed evasive action. Twenty-two years on, when the 1974 party toured, their manager was Lt.-Col. Hemu Adhikari, who had been one of Fred's victims on that memorable day. The two

He missed and took a blow in that sensitive area ...

bumped into each other again in the bar at Old Trafford, where Fred's first words were: 'Hello, Colonel, I'm glad to see you've got your colour back.'

Back in 1959, Polly Umrigar paid Fred the sort of compliment that any fast bowler would appreciate. Umrigar was a very fine player indeed, appearing in fifty-nine tests and scoring 3,631 runs for an average of 42.22. As he also enjoyed the relatively rare distinction of scoring 172 not out and taking five wickets for 107 against West Indies in Port of Spain in the 1961–2 series, he was clearly no mug with either bat or ball.

On the morning of the Yorkshire match at Bramall Lane, however, he suddenly decided he could not play because of a back strain. At the same time, Fred was also being declared unfit with ankle trouble and, when news of his indisposition reached the Indian camp, Umrigar stretched himself a couple of times and decided that he might just make it after all. Meanwhile, back in the treatment room, Fred was having his ankle strapped up and eventually it was agreed he could turn out, whereupon Umrigar suffered a relapse!

Perhaps, therefore, it is not surprising that Fred has become larger than life, being kept in the public spotlight as a member of the very popular *Test Match Special* team, who have popularised cricket to the extent that housewives listen intently to their coverage of the big matches. In the circumstances, it is not difficult to believe a little story about Fred being stopped for speeding. The police car, it is rumoured, had to chase him for many miles at high speed before at last they attracted his attention and got him to stop. 'Why, it's Freddy Trueman,' said the officer when he arrived to take down the particulars. 'You were really travelling. You must have been driving as fast as you bowl.' 'Nah,' snorted an outraged Fred. 'If I had have been, you wouldn't have seen my tail for dust.'

In a match at Park Avenue, Fred, who more often

than not found plenty of assistance in the pitch, beat one particular batsman with agonising frequency outside the off stump. This sequence prompted some lively exchanges. 'I don't know what you brought that bat out with you for,' exclaimed the disappointed Trueman. 'Try bowling it a bit slower, I might get some wood on it then,' responded the batsman, who had been to university and fancied his chances as a wit. 'Nay, if I bowl it any slower, it won't get there at all,' came the cutting rejoinder.

When Fred brought one back off the seam, the batsman was all at sea and there was a big appeal for lbw. The ball would definitely have knocked out the middle stump, but the umpire said 'Not out' firmly. 'He played that, Fred,' he said. 'Just got an inside edge and that saved him. It was out otherwise.' 'Aye, that's right,' agreed the aggrieved bowler. 'But that's what's wrong wi' t' laws.'

Not being given to bouts of false modesty, Trueman wanted to call his biography *T' Definitive Volume on t' Finest Bloody Fast Bowler that Ever Drew Breath*. With an eye for impact and economy, the publishers relied instead simply on *Fred*. Really, there was nothing more to say.

Not that Fred, whatever he might think, was the only fast bowler to chill the blood of the opposition. Harold Larwood, the hero or villain – depending on how you look at it and where you were born – of the Bodyline argument between England and Australia, caused concern among batsmen in every corner of the cricket world. Like Fred, he could bat a bit as well, so he was equipped to look after himself, as he proved in a match between Nottinghamshire and Northamptonshire.

Nobby Clark, of Northamptonshire, could be a bit lively and liked to let go a few bouncers just to remind people he was about. Well, he dropped too short at both Larwood and his formidable bowling colleague Bill Voce, who were clearly annoyed by this breach of the unwritten traditions of the period. Clark eventually had to take his turn at the wicket, of course, and he did not have the ability to deal with the situation he had created. The first ball from Larwood leapt head-high, flicking the edge of the bat on the way to first slip, who picked it up on the bounce. 'Well bowled,' said Clark, departing towards the pavilion. 'Not out, it didn't carry,' said the umpire. 'It was near enough for me,' insisted Clark.

All hostile fast bowling is not necessarily intentional. It is possible for some young quickie, anxious to do well, to lose a bit of control and the result is sometimes spectacular. After all, the batsman has a reasonable chance of dealing with a bouncer that he is at least half-expecting. When it comes about by accident he can be taken off-guard. I was standing in a very important championship clash between Derbyshire and Nottinghamshire at Trent Bridge in 1987 when Devon Malcolm got himself into a spot of bother.

Every match is, of course, important, but this had an added significance in that Nottinghamshire were pressing hard for the title. The batsmen had been very much on top. Derbyshire made 339, with their captain Kim Barnett top scoring on 130 and Nottinghamshire were well on their way to 389 in reply.

Devon is one of the nicest lads you could meet in a long day's march, but he was firing on all cylinders in his efforts to get a wicket. Four bouncers went whistling down in the space of seven balls. 'Come on, Devon, we can't have this,' I informed him. 'You must keep the ball further up. The odd bouncer is all right, but not all these.' 'I am very sorry, it won't happen again,' he agreed. A few overs later he hit Clive Rice on the arm with a wild full toss. Again he apologised profusely. 'It slipped, I didn't mean to do it,' he said, and I believed him. 'Right, now,' I replied. 'You've had your sighters above and below the target. Let's see if you can hit a decent length.' Happily he did just that.

Another mishap involved Peter Broughton, a pace

bowler who appeared briefly for Yorkshire in 1956. He actually took sixteen wickets at 22.81 each, so he didn't do too badly by any means. In one match against Sussex, at Bradford, Billy Sutcliffe, the captain, gave him the new ball in the absence of the more established stars such as Fred Trueman. Very well aware of the honour, Peter decided to operate from the old football stand end and came steaming up to the stumps concentrating all his energy into the delivery stride. Neither he nor anyone else is exactly sure what happened next.

When he let the ball go, it turned into the beamer to end all beamers. It whistled like a bullet past the amazed batsman Don Smith and over the wicketkeeper's head. Those who have watched cricket at the old Park Avenue ground will recall that the pavilion area was separated from the playing area by a substantial wall. Well, the ball cleared this, too, scattering the crowd immediately behind the wicket. This caused a good deal of consternation and someone waved a white handkerchief in mock surrender.

I doubt if Peter could have repeated the feat even if he had wanted to, for it certainly could not have been easy to clear the wall with a proper bowling action. The general feeling remained that the ball had slipped, but even so he might well have received a quiet word from the umpire.

The one thing about pace bowling is that it gives you a quick, clean death – more or less! – while spinners can inflict slow torture. There is nothing worse for a player than being unable either to cope with the turning ball or to get out decently. It may sound silly, but there are instances when a batsman simply cannot give his wicket away no matter how hard he tries, short of deliberately knocking over his own stumps.

Mushtaq Mohammad, one of the prolific Pakistan cricketing family, and Yorkshire's Arthur Robinson were the principal figures in a funny exchange at Bradford in 1977. Mushtaq took six for 63 in Yorkshire's first innings as they built a decent lead and wanted every possible run. The contest got bogged down when Robinson and Geoff Cope put on 38 for the last wicket, largely because Mushtaq was spinning his leg breaks and googlies so much.

Robinson, a persistent and reliable left-arm seamer, struggled manfully but, like the Ancient Mariner just about stopped one in three. While Robinson could not make reliable contact, Mushtaq failed to find either the edge of the bat or the stumps. 'For goodness' sake, Arthur,' he pleaded at the end of one over, 'we are beginning to look silly.' 'It's not my fault,' complained Robinson. 'Bowl straight.' So it went on until, after beating the bat with six successive deliveries, Mushtaq grinned and shouted: 'It's all right, you can open your eyes now. I've finished.'

||| 6 |||

'Yes, No, Wait; Sorry'

Colin Cowdrey turned up at a cricket function wearing a new tie. It carried the three lions of England with the number 75 underneath. 'That's a smart tie,' someone said. 'But what does the 75 mean?' 'Oh, that's the number of batsmen Geoff Boycott has run out in Test cricket.' Cowdrey said with a smile. At the same gathering, Peter Parfitt sported similar neckwear, except that his tie carried the number 5. 'That represents the people Geoff Boycott has not run out in Test cricket,' he said.

Being run out, particularly through a misunderstanding, is the worst possible way to be dismissed in cricket. If it is not your fault – and not many people own up – the feeling of frustration is so much the greater. As everyone is aware, Geoff gained a reputation for being difficult to run with, and it was ironic that his last first-class innings – against Northamptonshire at Scarborough in September 1986 – should end in a run out when he and Jim Love got their wires crossed.

I had first-hand experience of Geoff's single-minded approach to this complicated matter. When I played with Barnsley in the Yorkshire League my opening partner was Michael Parkinson and we were close to being the best pair in the area at the time. Parky did well enough to be invited to the county nets, so we were both senior to G. Boycott, a schoolboy who came around number six in the order.

I remember all too clearly being on 49 against Sheffield United at Shaw Lane, Barnsley. I turned the off-spinner

... a schoolboy who came in around number six in the order.

safely through a gap on the leg side down towards the mid-wicket boundary and was really looking forward to a big collection from a good-sized crowd as I set off for the easy single, calling: 'Come on, one,' almost as a matter of course. Geoff remained calmly achored in his crease. 'Keep running, Dickie,' he said as I reached his end, 'Keep running all the way to the pavilion.'

To say I was displeased would be an understatement and since then Geoff has upset one or two, although his weakness in this area has been exaggerated. Another dodgy runner was the great Denis Compton – the only man, so his famous friend Bill Edrich told me, to wish his partner luck as he set off for a run. Another of Compton's colleagues said that when Denis called for a single that was merely the basis for negotiation.

It should, however, be a simple process, certainly with the openers who operate together on a regular basis, and they say that Herbert Sutcliffe and Percy Holmes hardly needed to exchange more than a glance. Yorkshire's most prolific first-wicket pair both knew well enough whether a run was available and acted accordingly.

Similarly, David Hunter, the long-serving wicketkeeper, who shared in what was for a long time Yorkshire's record last wicket stand with Lord Hawke, claimed a ready understanding with his captain. 'We never needed to call each other when we set off,' he said. 'If there was a run we ran and said nothing about it at all.' He is alleged to have added: 'In any case, I always thought it was his Lordship's privilege to speak first.'

Even with the best will in the world, mistakes can occur and judgments become clouded. Two minds can react to the same situation in catastrophically different ways. Take for instance the case of Brian Close, who had a painful experience with Richard Hutton as his companion in confusion. Close was attempting to obtain most of the strike as he chased runs with the intention of setting a target on the last day of a championship match. He forced the ball away on the leg side and charged down the pitch. Hutton, meanwhile, watching to see if the stroke had beaten mid-on, remained in his ground and was surprised to discover his captain standing alongside him and breathing heavily down his neck.

With an anguished cry, Closey turned to go back. As luck would have it, the fieldsman became distracted by all the shouting and fumbled his pick-up. This allowed Closey time to hurl himself into the crease at the striker's end a fraction ahead of the return. Picking himself up and dusting himself down, Brian stormed up to Hutton. 'Why the heck didn't you run, you know I wanted to keep the bowling,' he roared. Unperturbed, Hutton listened to this and a lot more before politely saying: 'It's quite all right with me, skipper, but if you do want to bat at both ends I suggest you contact Lord's to see if you can get the laws changed.'

Richard, with his impressive academic background, rarely failed to come up with an apt expression. After listening to a long account from Fred Trueman about some of the wickets he had taken and some of the superb deliveries he had unleashed, he quietly asked: 'Tell me, Fred, did you ever just bowl a straight one?'

Even then he did not have the last word. 'Aye, it were a full toss,' retorted Fred. 'It went through Peter Marner like a dose of salts and knocked his middle pole clean out.'

Peter Marner, as it happens, played with Lancashire and two other representatives of Yorkshire's Roses foes – Alan Wharton and Cyril Washbrook – had a slight difference in running between the wickets.

Washbrook established himself as one of the outstanding openers after the Second World War, becoming linked with Len Hutton in a high-class partnership which prospered against some superb Australian bowling and would have been even more successful in less demanding times. Wharton must have been regarded as the junior member of the partnership on the day in question, but he grew in stature as he steadily approached a well-constructed century. On 99 he was called for a risky single by Washbrook and turned it down, causing considerable alarm. 'When I call, you should run,' said Cyril. 'I'm a very good judge of these things.' Wharton stood his ground manfully. 'That may be, but when I'm on 99 I am the best judge in the world of a single,' he claimed.

The question of financial reward and, for that matter, averages cannot be ignored when running. My old friend Fred Jakeman recounted an experience which underlined this point. When playing as a professional for a league club, he had the misfortune to arrive on the ground rather late due to unforseen circumstances. Luckily Fred's captain had won the toss and batted, so that there was no problem. But Fred had to sit in the pavilion with his pads on while a quite stylish amateur plundered some weak bowling. The frustrating thing, from Fred's point of view, what that a very big crowd sat basking in the sun, ready to be generous in contributing to the first collection of the day.

The stylish amateur moved smoothly into the forties, but his partner did the decent thing from Fred's point of view and got out. Fred marched purposefully to the middle, mentally counting the pounds, shillings and pence that were likely to be forthcoming. With better luck, he might have played for England at some time, for he got quite a few runs for Northamptonshire. Working on the assumption that the amateur would do as he was told, Fred worked the bowling to suit his purposes and got to 50 first, allowing his 'leg man' only three balls while making his runs off only 25 deliveries. 'It were a nice collection,' he recalled, 'and it had to go to the professional, didn't it?'

Less successful was Ted Peate, the famous Yorkshire

left-arm spinner of the last century. During the England v Australia Tests of 1884, he became anxious about the fallibility of Stanley Christopherson in the course of a last-wicket stand. 'Steady, Mr Christopherson, I'm getting ten bob a run,' he cried. But his plea fell on stony ground. Christopherson fell to a catch in the next over.

There have been many eccentric runners, although happily the most notorious have seldom batted together. Imagine, if you like, Boycott and Compton debating the pros and cons of a sharp single. Two who did find themselves in confusing partnership were Sam Cook and Bomber Wells, Gloucestershire's spin twins in the 1950s and 60s. I knew Sam well because he turned to umpiring after his playing career, which began with a wicket with his first ball in first-class cricket. Sam told me of a muddle when he and Bomber had got into one of their terrible tangles, finding themselves stranded in mid-wicket as the fielding side dissolved in mirth and leisurely completed the run-out. 'Look, Bomber,' said Sam, 'You ought to call.' 'Oh, all right,' replied his unabashed team-mate. 'Heads.'

The fact that cricket laws allow for another player to run for an injured batsman adds an extra dimension to the relationship between the strikers out in the middle. It sounds a bit improbable to me, but there is a documented account of Sam and Bomber both needing a runner while in partnership. This had to be a recipe for disaster – and so it proved. According to the unofficial history of the event, Sam played the ball away and instinctively set off for a single. So did Bomber at the other end. Meanwhile both runners, fulfilling their respective roles in the drama, also began to run. Realising his error, Sam turned to go back, his action persuading Bomber and Bomber's runner that he had decided there wasn't a single. They too turned to retrace their steps.

Sam's runner had advanced a good deal further up the pitch than the other three before he decided to get into step, as it were. He began to retrace his steps, by which time, with all the shouts of 'Yes, come on,' 'No go back' and 'Wait a minute' echoing backward and forward, all concerned were totally confused.

Somehow defying all logic, the four of them eventually came together in the middle of the pitch and then, like carriage horses in harness, trotted briskly in the same direction.

Exerting a good deal of will power, a member of the fielding side managed to stop rolling about long enough to break the wicket. The appeal was really superfluous and when it came the umpire, scratching his head, said: 'One of you is out, there's no doubt about that, but which one is a mystery to me. You'd better sort it out among yourselves.'

I suppose that one-day cricket, although strongly criticised in many quarters, has definitely improved two areas of play – fielding and running between the wickets – and there is no doubt that players in the 1980s are much fitter than most of their predecessors. When there was only the championship, and events proceeded at a gentler pace, batsmen could afford to take a breather here and there. Thus, after one hectic spell in the heat of the day during a game in Australia, a breathless Ken Barrington suggested to Fred Titmus: 'Let's cut out some of the quick singles for a bit.' 'OK, Ken, we'll cut out yours,' decided his partner.

That, by the way, raises another point. It takes two to run a single, so the fitness of both men has to be taken into account. Some youngsters can be down the pitch in the twinkling of an eye, while others take a bit of time to get started.

Still, the best advice of all probably came from Wilfred Rhodes, who merely said: 'When I'm coming I say "yes", when I'm not, I say "no".'

... like carriage horses in harness, trotted briskly in the same direction.

||| 7 |||

Jokers Wild

Cricket is a game that has always been packed with character and there is still plenty about today. The modern players may be different in many ways from the old-timers, but men like Ian Botham, Mike Brearley, Allan Lamb, Bob Willis, Dennis Lillee and so many others are instantly recognized figures in their own right. They have a relationship with the public and it does not matter a jot whether it is always a favourable one. The fact is that they stand out and attract attention. In the 1979 season, for instance, Bob Willis bowled just 134 overs for War-wickshire and claimed nine wickets in the full championship campaign, although earning his England place in the Test series to demonstrate that he had lost none of his fire power. When he opened the attack in one of his rare appearances for the county at Edgbaston, a member, brandishing a scorebook, stood up to enquire in a loud voice: 'Bowler's name, please?' Even Bob, who normally screws his concentration up tight to get in the mood for fast bowling, had to smile at that.

David Bairstow, the tough Yorkshire wicketkeeper, who proved virtually indestructible as he overcame one injury after another to keep his place in the side, is a larger-than-life personality with a ready wit. As we have noted, life on the county circuit can be very demanding. Yorkshire had endured a long hot spell in the field, with play continuing right through the last hour on the final day, before driving to Southampton for a fixture with Hampshire. It was very late indeed when the party staggered into their hotel, so no-one had had much rest when they reported to the ground next morning. They lost the toss and faced another punishing slog under the sun. So Bairstow stretched himself out on a bench in the dressing room to snatch a few precious minutes of peace and quiet.

It was not to be. An eager colleague strolled across, bat and ball in hand. 'Come on, Blue,' he said, 'You're the only one left to give me a knock-up.' With a resigned air, Bairstow got to his feet. 'OK,' he agreed. 'And if you bring me a bucket of sand I'll sing you the Desert Song while I'm at it.'

The late and much-missed Tony Nicholson, who died at a tragically early age, was another typical Yorkshireman – blunt, generous and totally absorbed by cricket. Back in 1974, when Ian Botham was just a big lad starting in the game with Somerset, Yorkshire appeared in a Sunday League game at Bath. The contest built up to an exciting climax, with Bairstow and Nicholson Yorkshire's last pair, Botham the bowler and 5 runs needed for victory. The situation demanded a mid-wicket conference between the batsmen and I gather that the conversation went something like this. Bairstow: 'I have to get the strike, so whatever happens to the first ball I shall be running. You run as hard as you can.' Nicholson: 'Right. Whatever happens I'll run.'

Having settled that issue, they returned to their ends, Nich to face the bowling of the youthful Botham, who whistled one past his off stump to wicketkeeper Jim Parks. Off went Bairstow like a sprinter out of the blocks at the non-striker's end. Getting to halfway he realised that Nich had no intention of moving, so he applied the brakes and made some attempt to get back. Nich, meanwhile, suddenly sprang to life and embarked on a run himself. He had got only a few strides when Parks calmly broke the wicket to give his side a 'short-head' victory. As they stomped their way through the cheering fans. Bairstow asked: 'What were you doing?' 'Sorry, Blue,' said Nich, 'I forgot what we'd agreed.'

Nich thoroughly enjoyed the social side of the first-class round, so Scarborough stood high on the list of his favourite grounds. There is a relaxed atmosphere at North Marine Road and the town lends itself to a spot of holiday-making at the end of the season. The Festival has been marked by a few bizarre incidents including the bailing out of a top amateur batsman so that he could continue his innings. His incarceration followed a hectic night on the tiles.

Towards the end of the 1974 season, Yorkshire staged a championship engagement with Kent at Scarborough and Colin Cowdrey decorated the match with a century of the highest class. Even the partisan crowd admired the elegant progress as the ball was persuaded towards the boundary. Nich, with an unquenchable spirit, manfully shouldered his share of the burden on a baking afternoon, doing as well as anyone on a pitch guaranteed to break all but the stoutest bowler's heart.

Throughout Barrie Leadbeater, yet another York-shireman to move on to umpiring, stood at first slip. Barrie had a very fine technique himself and was ready to see the best in others. 'Oh, good shot, Colin,' he murmured whenever an excellently-timed stroke sent the ball racing over the parched turf. All nice friendly stuff, but Nich clearly thought it out of place. 'If I hear you say "well played" once more, Leaders, I'll kick you up the backside and that's a promise,' he warned. 'Sorry,' apologised Barrie, 'but you must admit it's marvellous to watch.' 'Marvellous?' exploded the perspiring seamer hotly. 'Let me tell you, I'd just as soon walk all the way back to Leeds with a nail up in my shoe as suffer him for another bloody minute.'

In that same season, Yorkshire lost by eight wickets to

Middlesex at Middlesbrough on an Acklam Park pitch that gave more than expected help to the spinners. Fred Titmus enjoyed himself as Yorkshire were dismissed cheaply and the match turned on a spectacular innings from Norman Featherstone. Working on the theory that he might as well make as many runs as possible before he got the inevitable unplayable delivery, he thrashed the bowling all over the field. Yorkshire were simply helpless and in the bar afterwards, one or two of the Middlesex lads were suitably sympathetic. 'There wasn't much you could do about that,' said one. 'Norman chanced his arm and got away with it. He smashed it about so well he didn't give even the slightest chance.' 'Oh, I don't know about that,' interrupted Nich. 'I distinctly saw a chap in a grey pullover miss him on the back row of the seats at mid-wicket.' A pause. 'Mind you, he was standing on the bench at the time.'

I haven't come across many people who actually describe Geoff Boycott as a character, but you could never ignore him, and he did become the hero in a thousand legends. Like the one about him having breakfast in the team hotel in London. Geoff is a very careful eater and has even discussed diet with Barbara Cartland, the internationally respected writer of romantic fiction, who claims she has a letter from him attributing his run-making feats to her advice. On the day in question, Boycs was still eating when a smartly dressed young man approached his table. 'Excuse me,' he said, 'but I wonder if I could ask you a very big favour.'

Being accustomed to this sort of scene, Boycs tried to ignore the intrusion, but the young man persisted. 'I am actually on the short list for a job with the BBC in their sports service and tonight I am dining in this hotel with the head of the department. You don't know me, of course, but I wonder if you happen to be in the dining room if you could possibly just walk past and say something like

"Hello, Ian" and carry on. It would make a very big impression.'

Boycott promised nothing, but he had a good day and made a nice steady century, so he was in a buoyant mood when he returned to the hotel. After relaxing and going over the whole of the innings in his mind, he decided to have a meal and, sure enough, there in the dining room was the young man who had sought his help at breakfast. Well, he thought, it can't do any harm to give him a helping hand, so he made it in his way to pass the table where his new-found friend was deep in conversation with a distinguished-looking gentleman. 'Hello, Ian, how are you?' asked Geoff, pausing only slightly to create the right impression. 'Not now, Geoff, can't you see I'm busy,' came the terse reply.

Supposedly, there was also the time when Boycott is alleged to have got into conversation with a pretty receptionist at another hotel. 'Look,' he is reported to have said, 'why don't we have dinner together tonight?' He received a favourable reply, but suddenly changed his mind, adding: 'No, I'll be batting all day tomorrow. We'd better make it some other night.'

Yet another Boycott yarn concerns Bradford Park Avenue, where a group of senior citizens were watching him complete a flawless century. 'By gum,' opined one, 'I reckon our Geoff must be the best batsman in the world. Just look at yon shot through mid-wicket. That takes some playing, I can tell you.'

So it went on as the runs came, each stroke being duly appreciated. 'There's times when you think he'll never get out,' suggested a member of the party. 'I shouldn't be surprised if he were still batting when he's fifty.' 'Aye,' agreed another voice. 'But sometime he'll have to bow to Anno Domini.'

This stopped the conversation dead, causing a puzzled frown on the assembled faces. 'Nay, let's talk sense,' ventured one man at last. 'Them Italians can't play cricket, so how's one of them going to get him out?'

There might be a lot of arguments about the value of one-day cricket, but it cannot be seriously disputed that the limited-overs competitions have improved the standard of fielding out of all recognition. It used to be said that the great Yorkshire team of the late 1930s maintained brilliant standards in the field, but their dynamic captain, Brian Sellers – 'Crackerjack' to his men – admitted to me a few years ago: 'We were a long way behind the worst fielding side today. We took the catches all right before the war, but we did not save anything like the runs they do now and we certainly never did any diving on the boundary edge just to turn four into three.'

Some of the chasing and the diving stops which are part and parcel of the modern game spotlight the tremendous athleticism of those taking part, while physical training sessions are part of the daily schedules. You can even see the odd umpire running round the ground if you get there early enough. Alan Whitehead and Kevin Lyons often go through their paces.

One man who has never got to grips with this development is David Shepherd. He is, of course, built for comfort rather than speed and he has never been one to take too much exercise, preferring rather to save his energy. In one of his last seasons with Gloucestershire he discovered to his horror on reporting for pre-season training in April that the club had arranged a series of long cross-country runs. Despite his protests, he had to take part, but from the first found the going much too hard.

Soon he fell a long way behind the rest of the field. A number of his colleagues were on their way back while he was still on the outward leg. As desperation set in, Shep came across a milk float, driven by a cricket enthusiast. 'You don't happen to be going anywhere near the county ground, I suppose?' asked Shep. 'As a matter of fact, I've about another street to do and then I'm going straight back past there, so you can have a lift with pleasure,' said the milkman.

That suited Shep down to the ground and when his weary team-mates arrived back, he had had a shower and was handing out pints of milk. 'Well, I had to buy something after he'd been so nice to me,' he explained. After that, I gather he had a standing order with the milkman for a few days!

Ian Botham is never far to seek when there is a bit of horseplay going on. You have to keep a wary eye on him all the time and most of his playing colleagues have, at some time or another, found themselves pushed in the swimming pool at some hotel or had their clothes hidden or thrown in the water.

He is, in fact, literally larger than life. When in Australia, he was playing in a match in Newcastle, where he indulged in a bout of his customary big-hitting. The ball flew all over the ground as he hammered the bowling. The match was being televised, so he provided great entertainment for a very big audience. One chap was watching in a house next to the ground and, according to local information, Both's biggest hit sailed through his window and smashed the set on which he was watching play. That must be unique.

These modern characters are following in the footsteps of such as George Macaulay, who hated batsmen with all his being from 1920 to 1935, bitterly grudging every run they managed to steal from him. Years later an admirer happened to take the opportunity, when introduced to Macaulay, of congratulating him on one of his outstanding returns. 'I saw you take seven for 13 against Derbyshire at Chesterfield in 1925,' he said proudly. 'I must say you bowled superbly.' 'Aye,' Macaulay acknowledged, 'Then you know it should have been seven for 9 but for that bad misfield at mid-on.'

Both's biggest hit sailed through his window and smashed the set on which he was watching play.

Yorkshiremen have always taken these things seriously. Macaulay also filled the leading role in a game in which an amateur, fielding close to the wicket, held a very smart catch. He received a passing nod of approval, but no more. Seeking to underline the merit of his effort, he walked up to Macaulay and, holding out his arms, said: 'With these hands, Macaulay, I can catch pigeons.' As if to prove the point, he did well to share in another dismissal shortly afterwards. This time the bowler completely ignored him. Not to be outdone, the amateur again waved his arms before him. 'What did I tell you, Macaulay, with these hands I can help you to win this match,' he claimed.

Sadly, his luck ran out and a third chance went to ground. It had not been too easy, but Macaulay could not contain his anger. Walking up to the offender, he grabbed his wrists and shouted: 'With these hands, why don't tha strangle thissen?'

In the demanding circumstances of the Yorkshire side, only senior members were generally allowed to field in the slips. The position carried a significance in the order of things, so that Norman Yardley, as a young man, was a shade taken aback to be put there fairly soon in his career.

'Nah then,' Arthur Mitchell greeted his arrival, 'what are you doing here? I hope tha's got something interesting to talk about.'

Mitchell – 'Ticker' to all and sundry – did not appear to enjoy life very much. He gave nothing away as a batsman and went on, as county coach, to frighten the life out of generations of boys hoping to make it as county players. If you could survive a net session with 'Ticker' Mitchell, you could survive anything. His colleagues also came in for their share of stick.

Ellis Robinson understandably thought he had done quite well when he took a quite brilliant catch close to the wicket, hurling himself through the air like a goalkeeper to clutch the ball inches from the turf as he fell heavily.

'Well held,' congratulated the batsman as he turned away, and the spectators applauded enthusiastically. Robinson lay for a moment, the wind knocked out of him by the fall, but as he rolled over to regain his feet, Mitchell prodded him with the toe of his boot. 'Gerrup, tha's makin' an exhibition of thissen,' he snapped.

A distinctly more cheerful member of a truly brilliant Yorkshire team before the Second World War, Arthur Wood, contributed endlessly to the humour of cricket. A naturally bouncy man, he was never lost for words, even in what he may well have thought was his darkest hour. He made his Test debut in 1938 against the Australians at Lord's, but he had to dash from Scarborough to take his place in the team and the only available transport happened to be a taxi. The fare turned out to be very large indeed and Wood, on joining the other members of the England line-up, felt he could easily have bought a second-hand car for the same money.

While still recovering from this shock, he got involved in a small group at the bar and decided to celebrate his selection by buying a round of drinks. No sooner had he got 'in the chair', however, than two or three more joined his little band, so that the waiter had a substantial order. Staggering under the weight of his tray, he arrived and distributed the drinks, informing Wood of the price. It was a lot of money and, as the unhappy victim fumbled in his pocket, the waiter added: 'Don't forget me, sir.' He was doomed to disappointment. 'Eh lad,' said Wood as he counted out the exact sum, 'I'll remember you for the rest of my life.'

He also had good reason to recall another incident – or at least his team-mates had. Arthur had to attend a very formal dinner, attended by some influential and important guests. He enjoyed it well enough, but when questioned next day admitted that he had suffered acute indigestion. 'I had to eat quickly to keep up with the chap next to me,' he said. 'Surely you could have kept to your own pace, there wasn't a prize for finishing first,' said someone. 'That wasn't the point,' said Arthur. 'There were so many knives, forks and spoons about that I didn't want to be left to make any decisions of my own.'

While we are talking about Arthur, I have to tell another little tale about his amiable nature. Yorkshire were playing Cambridge University at Fenner's and, although the opposition contained one or two useful performers, Yorkshire were not under any pressure. They were mainly interested in some gentle practice. The young Cambridge opener had done quite well in the course of a brief innings when Bill Bowes found the edge and Arthur took the catch. The bowler appealed confidently and the umpire's decision was no more than a formality, but Arthur did not join in. 'That's the first time I haven't heard you ask for a catch,' said Bill. 'Aye well, I were having such an interesting chat wi' t' lad that I wouldn't have minded him hanging about for a bit longer,' confessed the friendly wicketkeeper.

Sport has not always been very rewarding. It was, no doubt, an enjoyable way of earning a small living, but until recently the returns left a lot to be desired. Perhaps this is why in Yorkshire, where things could be hard anyway, we have tended to link cricket with money so often. I like the story about Luke Greenwood, from Lascelles Hall, in the last century. W. G. Grace hit him out of the ground, and at the time it was the custom to give a shilling to anyone who returned a lost ball. After a brief delay this one was recovered by a little old lady, who toddled out to the wicket with it and offered it to Greenwood. He would have nothing to do with her. 'Nah,' he said. 'Yon's him that hit it, you mun go to him for t' brass.' Even the doctor had no answer to this and paid up with a smile.

One league professional I heard of always made it his

business to look for a one-armed man on every ground. This unusual habit caused much amusement, but he explained: 'I like to know if there's one about. If there is, I'll give him a couple of bob to take my collection.'

On a similar theme, Tom Emmett, our old pal from Halifax, had a narrow escape after taking eight for 22 to beat Surrey at the Oval in 1881. The crowd tried to carry him off shoulder high, but he wriggled free, crying: 'Nay, for goodness sake, tha'll have all t' brass rolling out of my pockets.'

I doubt, though, if anybody in the world has had so many adventures as Brian Close, who says a cricket ball can't hurt you because it is not in contact with the body long enough. I can find plenty to give him an argument, but I have to admit he has walked away from hundreds of scrapes without any damage. He walked through a plate glass door in a hotel and merely blinked like a character from a Tom and Jerry cartoon, while his courage in fielding almost on the edge of the bat is a talking point whenever players meet.

Even the formidable Fred Trueman let go the occasional loose delivery and a rare long hop gave Gloucestershire batsman Martin Young scope, as he thought, to pick up four easy runs. He middled a fierce pull, but the ball bounced off the side of Brian's head into the hands of slip. Brian never gave it another thought. He just got on with the game. But a spectator felt moved to check on his well-being at the close of play. 'I'm all right,' said Closey. 'But what if it had hit you between the eyes?' asked the amazed admirer. 'Oh that would have been different,' admitted Brian. 'The catch would most likely have gone to cover.'

If anything, Brian lacked patience. He wanted to get at the opposition and hammer them into the ground. As a consequence, he set very high standards and it is just as well that he enjoyed the luxury of a strong side around him.

Even then, not everything went right for them. After a poor morning session in the field, Brian decided to give his men a pep talk during the luncheon interval. 'There are three things we've got to do,' he stormed. 'The bowlers must get their act together and cut out the rubbish that's been sent down this morning. Secondly, the fielders have got to smarten up. We've been giving runs away all over the place, so let's go out there and do the job.'

'By the way, skipper, what's the third thing,' asked Jimmy Binks as they marched out into the afternoon sunshine. 'Oh, I don't know, you think of something,' snapped Brian.

Closey also gained something of a reputation as a dangerous driver and he had one or two accidents. Having picked up a car, he arrived at the ground with a scratch down the side and less than twenty miles on the clock. 'Well,' pointed out Ray Illingworth, 'I see they've got to know you at the garage. They are providing a new car already knocked about a bit to save you the trouble.'

Brian could play any ball game superbly well. He might easily have been a professional soccer star, did well as an amateur boxer and can pot profitably at snooker, but really excels at golf, which he plays to a low handicap left- and right-handed. There's not many can do that. All the same, he can be a bit short-tempered and the odd club has been known to go flying through the air at moments of tension. One got stuck in a tree, so Closey hurled another up in a vain attempt to dislodge it and ended up with two tangled in the branches. He had to climb the tree to get them back, much to the delight of a gathering audience.

Brian had a particularly bad round by his standards while playing with Don Mosey, the radio commentator. Amidst a good deal of muttering and grumbling, he steadily got worse. The climax came when he lost his temper completely and hurled his clubs and bag into a lake next to the fairway. 'That's it, I'm finished,' he snorted, striding

He had to climb the tree to get them back . . .

off towards the club house. Don and the two other members of the four-ball continued to the eighteenth. As they came off the course they noticed the distant figure of Closey, up to his knees in the water, obviously fishing about for his clubs. They strolled over to see what was happening. 'I thought you'd given up golf altogether,' said Don. 'So I have,' shouted Brian. 'But I've got to find the damned bag, my car keys are in it.'

Allan Jones, who bowled the brisk side of medium for Sussex, Somerset, Middlesex and Glamorgan before trying his hand as umpire, became the butt of good-natured comments from the public because he grunted loudly every time he delivered the ball. But it did get him at least one wicket. In a fixture with Leicestershire he knocked back middle stump as Ray Illingworth took an uncharacteristic swing at a good-length ball. Illy was clearly very annoyed with himself when he reached the dressing room to meet the enquiring looks of his team. 'I know, I know,' he admitted, 'that was a lousy shot. But Jonah grunted so loudly that I thought it was the umpire calling no-ball.'

Anyone who has tried it will appreciate that captaincy is not as easy as it looks. There are plenty of experts ready to criticise from a distance and the good skipper has to have his mind on a mass of things, so I suppose that on balance batsmen have the better chance of doing the job well. This is not to say that bowlers can't be successful, but they do have their own game to concentrate on, and they have the problem of when to use themselves in the attack. The danger of being too cautious or too optimistic is obvious.

Tom Goddard, the outstanding Gloucestershire slow bowler, took over the captaincy of the side on a temporary basis during the late 1940s. Naturally, he put himself on, for he was certainly the county's most dangerous bowler, but it happened to be one of those days when nothing really went his way. He toiled on and on throughout the afternoon until at one point he turned to a colleague and complained: 'I don't know why the skipper doesn't take me off, I'm never going to get a wicket today.'

Fred Trueman had a slightly different reaction. While standing in for Brian Close, Fred got through a long spell without hitting his most effective rhythm and wicket-keeper Jimmy Binks volunteered the thought that a change might be needed. 'Aye,' agreed Fred, 'I reckon tha could be right. I'll try t' other end.'

||| 8 |||

In the News

Love them or hate them, the Press are always with us, and a lot of cricketers feel they have more influence over what the public think than any of the officials. There is a view that cricket writers have changed and that the development of tabloid newspapers, which take a lively approach to covering the news, sensationalises events.

That may be true to some extent, but it was not exactly yesterday that Emmott Robinson, that sage of Yorkshire, told one of the most famous cricket journalists of all time: 'Eh, Mr Cardus, I reckon tha's invented me.' Neville Cardus did produce some of the most colourful prose and entertained an awful lot of readers, which is exactly what many of the tabloid boys claim they do today.

I remember being shown a cutting of a report written by Cardus which concerned the Test match between England and Australia at Old Trafford in 1896. The great man's description, in referring to the end of the contest in which Tom Richardson, of Surrey, had bowled magnificently but in vain, went: 'He stood at the bowling crease, dazed. Could the match have been lost? His spirit protested. Could it be that the gods had looked on and permitted so much painful striving to go by unrewarded? His body still shook from the violent motion. He stood there like some animal baffled at the uselessness of great strength and effort in this world. A companion led him to the pavilion and there he fell wearily to a seat.' Cardus was not actually covering that particular- match and his piece appeared some years later. The accounts of those present were quite a bit different. One said: 'As I recall it, once the winning hit had been made, Tom ran like a stag to the pavilion and got down two pints in a flash.' Cardus, I understand, was only seven years old when the fixture was staged.

He did say, though, that those who wanted always to stick exactly to the truth were 'happy to kill a good story dead'. I am quite friendly with a few reporters who agree wholeheartedly with that sentiment. One of the most repeated legends insists that George Hirst instructed Wilfred Rhodes: 'We'll get them in singles,' when this pair came together against Australia at the Oval in 1902 needing 15 for victory. They did, in fact, almost do just that, but Rhodes said: 'If we could have got four fours it would have been finished a lot sooner.' (In fact, they did not stick to ones, though thirteen of Hirst's last fourteen scoring strokes were singles.)

I cannot imagine that today's writers would have missed the dramatic story of the first few overs in the fixture between Surrey and Essex at Leyton in 1925. The two captains, Percy Fender and Johnny Douglas, had had a disagreement and were not on good terms. The match was heading for a draw on the last day, with both sides having scored heavily. Just before the start, Fender discovered that the professionals in his ranks had been delayed in their charabanc on their way from London. Only he and another amateur, Alfred Jeacocke, were available for the resumption. Rather than concede the result they went out to field. The Essex batsmen played out a few maiden overs, making no attempt to score until the rest of the Surrey side turned up.

There is, significantly, no record of this passage of play either in the papers or in Wisden, but the facts of the case have been handed down by word of mouth from some who were present. Douglas is reputed to have said: 'We were playing to the strict rules of MCC.' The punch line belongs to Surrey wicketkeeper Herbert Strudwick, who is supposed to have commented on his arrival on the field: 'I hope there haven't been any byes.' That could well be true, for he had a real pride in his profession. Wicketkeepers regard byes as a comment on their ability. A league stumper, finding himself keeping to a new leg spinner whom he could not 'read', conceded two lots of four byes in the first over from the newcomer. Before the second, he clapped his gloves noisily together, then crouched down with his hands just by the offstump. 'See these gloves?' he shouted, 'Well, you had better hit them from now on, because they aren't going to move.'

I have had a personal example of fiction being a lot less interesting than fact. A photograph appeared in a local evening paper at the end of the Lord's Test match between England and Australia in 1985 showing Ian Botham leaving the field deep in conversation with me. The caption suggested we were discussing some key point in the day's events. Nothing could have been further from the truth.

We were not even talking about cricket at all. The subject of our little chat was Allan Clarke, the former Leeds United and England goal poacher. He, of course, is manager of Barnsley and was a big pal of Ian's when he was in charge at Scunthorpe. Both, you may recall, had a lively spell as an occasional footballer at the Old Show Ground and I was asking if he had any intention of trying his luck under Clarkie at Oakwell.

He told me he would be giving it a lot of thought, but I guess he was pulling my leg – fine, square, short or otherwise. One little secret Both did let slip, however, was that Clarkie presented him with a box of Mars bars whenever he scored a goal for Scunthorpe. I wonder if that was the reason Ian had to start watching his weight?

I won't say any more about that, though. If Both thinks I am having a joke at his expense, he'll get his own back by calling me Richard. It's surprising how many people

It's surprising how many people think Dickie is short for Richard.

think Dickie is short for Richard. In fact, I was christened Harold Denis Bird, but I soon became Dickie to all and sundry. I hate being called Richard, which is why Both, Geoff Boycott and one or two others will use the name when they want to get me going.

One of the difficulties for journalists – or so they keep telling me – is actually getting their reports through to the office. The invention of radio telephones and things like that has made life a lot easier for them, but not so long ago the men out on the road had to make all sorts of elaborate arrangements. Even in 1974 there could be snags.

It was in that year that Geoff Boycott lost his place in the England team and began a three-year exile. That business has been talked about often enough, but there was a funny story behind the scenes. A newspaper rushed a reporter to Bath, where Yorkshire were playing Somerset, and he booked into a small hotel on the Friday night. During the weekend he rushed about trying to find out exactly what was happening as Boycott withdrew from the game because of illness, and eventually, late on the Sunday evening, he managed to get a few words out of the man himself. This represented a scoop, so he hurried back to his bedroom to write up the interview and then picked up the telephone in his room. Nothing happened. He listened to the silence for several minutes before going downstairs in search of assistance.

After a good deal of shouting and banging, he managed to attract the attention of the night porter, a very elderly gentleman who promised to plug him through on the hotel switchboard. The newspaperman rushed back to his room and again picked up the telephone. Nothing. Several more minutes elapsed, so off he went again. The night porter was nowhere to be seen and once more it required a good deal of effort to bring him from his hiding place.

The journalist had by now lost his temper. 'Look, you

old dodderer, I need to make a telephone call and I need to make it now. Just pull yourself together and connect me or there'll be trouble.' The night porter did not reply, but put on his hat and coat and disappeared through the door. Not having the slightest idea how to work the switchboard, the reporter had to venture out into the night himself to find a public telephone and it took him a long time to accomplish what had seemed at the outset a simple task.

To make matters worse, it began to rain heavily while he was in the phone box so that he became soaked on his walk back to the hotel, arriving much the worse for wear at the entrance to be greeted by the manager. 'Are you the gentleman who has been having trouble with our telephone?' he was asked. 'I certainly am,' he replied, 'and I'm glad you are here in person to apologise. It simply isn't good enough.' 'Oh, I'm not here to apologise,' snapped the manager. 'I'm here to tell you to pack your bags and leave at once. My night porter will not return to his post until you have gone.' Taken aback, our hero queried: 'What ever happened to the old theory that the customer is always right?' 'That went out of fashion when I discovered that it is easier to get guests than night porters,' said the manager with a tone of crushing finality.

The longest-serving reporter that I have come across on the cricket circuit was Dick Williamson, from Bradford, who remained involved in one way and another for more than fifty years. He still made it his business to send out the scores from home matches when well turned eighty, and throughout he put a tremendous emphasis on accuracy. 'The scores must always be correct in every way, manner and means,' he insisted, and he went to great lengths to make sure there were no errors.

In 1980 Yorkshire met Sussex in a championship fixture at Headingley and, due to an accident, the visitors turned up in Leeds without their official scorer. An emergency

. . . he went to great lengths to make sure there were no errors.

replacement had to be found and play got under way with only Yorkshire's Ted Lester on duty. A wicket fell in the early stages, Bill Athey being caught at slip off Imran Khan. With no Sussex representative on the spot, a brief discussion took place between the Press and Lester before general agreement awarded the catch to Chris Waller. That was not good enough for Williamson. 'Guesswork is no answer,' he exclaimed. 'If no-one else can find out for certain, I can.'

He stamped his way down the long flight of steps which lead from the Press area at Headingley and was seen by his surprised colleagues climbing over the rails and marching onto the field. With Imran racing in, he approached third man to demand: 'Who took the catch?' The startled member of the Sussex ranks had no chance to answer, for an edge sent the ball racing in his direction. 'Get out of the way, mate,' he shouted as he did the necesary fielding. 'You've got to get off, you can't stand about here.' 'Never mind all that, sonny boy,' said Williamson. 'The agency scores go out all over the world and have to be spot on. It's more important that I get my job done properly than you save the odd runs.' So, in order to restore order, the name was produced. Yes, it was Waller!

A proper case of mistaken identity involved the Bedser twins Alec and Eric. There are those who claim they can tell one from the other, but I would not like to put money on guessing correctly myself. They are as near identical as makes no difference. They once accidentally fooled a hairdresser in a strange town. On a rain-soaked afternoon, with no prospect of play, Alec decided to nip out to have a hair cut. These little, everyday things can be a nuisance when you are involved in a busy round of matches, so he welcomed the opportunity. When he returned to the dressing room, the work of the hairdresser was much admired. 'That's one of the best hair cuts I've seen,' admitted Eric. 'I think I'll go while I can.' Having been given directions by his brother, he soon found the shop and marched in. 'I would like a nice, neat trim,' he said. 'Good grief,' exclaimed the hairdresser, 'Your hair does grow quickly! I'm surprised you can keep up with it.'

A slightly different case of mistaken identity occurred at Grace Road, Leicester. Ken Shuttleworth, the Lancashire and England pace bowler, had not had one of his best days, experiencing persistent uncertainty with his run-up. The *Daily Express* cricket man, Pat Marshall, gave him a bit of stick in his match report next day. The Lancashire lads did not hesitate to draw Ken's attention to the criticism and he rose to the bait, telling them that he intended to go and see this Pat Marshall and tell him a thing or two.

It so happened that the local freelance in those days, Bill King, often had the assistance of his wife, Celia. When the Lancashire players reached the dressing room, Mrs King happened to be making her way across the ground. Those on the balcony called for Ken and pointed her out. 'That's Pat Marshall,' they told him, 'she's been writing on cricket for years.' Off went Ken, only to hurriedly retrace his steps. 'I've had second thoughts,' he said. 'You can't talk sense to a woman about fast bowling.'

Much more recently, John Callaghan, of the *Yorkshire Evening Post* in Leeds, who has helped me to put together this collection of thoughts and stories, became involved in a similar incident. He was covering the Yorkshire–Nottinghamshire championship match at Middlesbrough in 1987, when, on the Monday morning, a little drama unfolded. Nottinghamshire opener Chris Broad, continuing his innings from the Saturday, received only five balls from Stuart Fletcher before returning to the pavilion. When Derek Randall took his place, John decided further enquiries were necessary, particularly as Broad was due to play for England in the First Test against Pakistan at Old Trafford on the following Thursday.

This sort of interview can be a bit tricky, so John was pleasantly surprised when he reached the Nottinghamshire dressing room. Broad hurried to greet him, saying: 'It hasn't taken you long to get round here.' 'I just wanted to check what was the matter,' John said, striking while the iron looked pretty warm. 'It's the thumb,' Broad explained, holding out the hand. 'It's all right up to a point, but I can't really grip the bat properly.' He continued to illustrate the point at some length. Impressed with all this cheerful co-operation, John stepped in with the crucial question. 'What about going for an x-ray?' 'Well,' came the reply, 'I think that's rather up to you, isn't it? You're the expert.' Flattered, but puzzled, John had to ask: 'Why me?' 'Because you are the doctor, aren't you.'

It is much less likely that famous personalities will be taken for someone else. Fame, though, can be fleeting. I remember once being in Barnsley when two people passed me in the street. 'There you are,' I overheard one of them saying. 'I told you that Test umpire Dickie Bird lived around here. That chap we've just seen used to be him.'

Then there was the case of Wilfred Rhodes. A very keen admirer persuaded him to attend a social function in his native Huddersfield. It was a very mixed gathering of minor local dignitaries and the proud host busied himself introducing his principal guest to all and sundry. Eventually he came to a scholarly lady. 'This is Mr Rhodes,' he said, pushing the great man forward to have his hand shaken yet again. Before Wilfred had chance to say anything, the lady trilled: 'My word, aren't you sunburned? I suppose it's all those hours in the open air on your exploring trips.' The silence which followed was broken when the penny at last dropped on the host. 'Madam,' he informed her, 'this is Wilfred, not Cecil.'

Press boxes are full of angry accounts of brushes with gatemen. Somehow, it appears, these part-time representatives of officialdom are born with a deep suspicion of their fellow men and, according to my newspaper contacts, those at Lord's can be very demanding. Even C. B. Fry, a notable autocrat of the Golden Age, fell foul of one diligent defender of the entrance there. Driving up in his Bentley, Fry discovered that he had no Lord's pass with him. A brief exchange of words with the gateman did not bring the desired result. 'Surely you have seen me play here many times,' suggested Fry. 'You must know who I am.' 'I know you all right,' said the gateman. 'And I have seen you bat, which is another reason why you can't come in without a pass.'

Broadcasting has increased, with ball-by-ball reports on the Test matches and big knockout finals, and the local radio stations also give the leagues plenty of air time. To do so, though, they have to use amateur commentators and members at the clubs, a system which can lead to complications.

Radio Leeds had the good idea of ringing round the grounds to pick up the latest on-the-spot news from as many places as possible, with the expert in the studio holding the whole operation together. Things went smoothly until he came to a club in the Bradford League. After checking the score, the linkman asked: 'Who is getting the runs for your side?' The helpful amateur stepped in with the information, 'George is going well. I can't see the scoreboard from here, but he must be almost fifty.' At that moment the sound of tremendous cheering could be heard down the line. 'And all the noise presumably means he's got there,' guessed the studio reporter. 'Oh no, that's nowt to do wi' t' match,' came the reply. 'Charlie's just dropped t' one-armed bandit.'

I still think Brian Johnston, the doyen of radio men, came out with two of the best unexpected funnies. They always make me laugh when I remember them. One came when he filled in a lull in the action by describing the field, concluding with: 'And there's Cowdrey in the slips, bottom in the air, legs apart, just waiting for a tickle.' The other had been 'in the wings' and could not be avoided during the West Indies tour of England in 1976 – 'The bowler's Holding, the batsman's Willey!'

||| 9 |||

Their Sporting Lives

The question anyone professionally involved with cricket is always asked is: 'What do you do in winter?' No-one is the least bit interested in what professional footballers do in summer, the assumption presumably being that, in company with everybody else, they take their holidays. I'm pretty busy 'out of season,' often going overseas to umpire and lecture, but whenever I can I watch my local soccer club, Barnsley.

What seems like too long ago, I appeared with their junior side and, as a teenager, nursed the ambition of playing both games at the highest level. After all, I did captain my school side, despite being the smallest player. Sadly, turning out for Barnsley YMCA, I damaged my knee, needed a cartilage operation and never returned to soccer at a serious level.

I have, however, always loved football and one of my best pals as a boy was the late Tommy Taylor, who went from Barnsley to Manchester United and died in that terrible Munich air disaster in 1958. I have had a very good relationship with all the lads down at Oakwell, training with the Barnsley squad, so it is not perhaps surprising that I enjoy cheering them on.

I suppose that Mike Parkinson has made Skinner Normington their best-known player with his articles in the newspapers. Skinner was the old-fashioned type of half-back, utterly dedicated and very hard in the tackle. When you played against him you knew you had been in a game.

A distinctly hesitant and inexperienced youngster, making his first appearance for Barnsley at full-back, soon found himself in trouble. The winger tricked him and cut inside, beating the full-back for pace before scoring a fine individual goal. 'Listen, son,' exploded Skinner, 'If you let that winger get inside you again I'm going to smack your head.' Anxiously seeking to justify himself, the boy spoke up: 'But he did get past you as well,' he ventured. 'Right,' said Skinner, 'now I am going to smack your head'. He did just that, but I suspect that if there is any truth in the legend, it would have been just a light tap to keep him in his place.

The fans probably loved it, assuming that the great Skinner was giving the novice a bit of encouragement. That reminds me, going back to cricket for a minute, of Johnny Wardle. Mike Cowan, a really useful medium-paced left-arm seamer, dropped a catch off Johnny, who responded a bit like Skinner, going up to put a consoling arm around the offender's shoulders. You could see the nods of approval in the seated ranks. The old professional offering a kindly word. In reality, Johnny had a painful hold on Mick's ear while he underlined very carefully the dire consequences of any further slips.

You could bet a week's wage that when the going got really tough, Skinner came into contact with the referee. Having left an opponent face down in the mud, he was penalised. 'Very late tackle that, just watch it,' warned the official as he awarded the free kick. 'Sorry, ref,' Skinner apologised. 'The old legs aren't what they used to be, I got there as soon as I could.'

Skinner represented the 'old school' in what he considered to be a man's game – playing hard and as fair as the circumstances allowed. One cricket umpire cast in the same mould was Arthur Jepson, my colleague in the famous Lancashire–Gloucestershire Gillette Cup semi-final at Old Trafford.

Not a lot of people remember this, but Arthur, as well as being a quality seam bowler with Nottinghamshire, had a long run as a goalkeeper in a strong Stoke City side shortly after the war, figuring in the same side as, for instance, the very great Neil Franklin, a prince among centre-halves. Stoke were drawn to meet Middlesbrough at Ayresome Park in the sixth round of the FA Cup and Jack Jennings was in the home team. Jack went on to become the Northamptonshire Cricket Club physio-therapist for many years, but then he was a solid, reliable wing half.

He told me that before the kick-off the Middlesbrough players felt that they could rattle Arthur a bit if they put him under a lot of pressure. It turned out to be a close contest, with no goals in the first half. With Arthur getting a bit of a buffeting, the score still stood at nil–nil deep into the second period when Middlesbrough got a corner. Jack went up for the cross with Arthur and dug him in the ribs with his elbow as they jumped. The ball went clear and Arthur decided that he had taken about enough for one afternoon, so he ran after Jack, who took to his heels up-field. Unfortunately for Stoke, the ball went to Wilf Mannion and he took full advantage of the empty net to score the only goal with a long shot. Whenever Jack and Arthur met on the cricket circuit they had a laugh about the incident, although, knowing Arthur so well, I bet he was angry with himself at the time.

During my days as a batsman with Leicestershire, I became very friendly with Ron Nicholls, a constant run-maker for Gloucestershire, who also happened to be a very good goalkeeper. There have been one or two keepers who also played cricket, and Ron had a regular spot for Bristol Rovers. When they came to Oakwell, I stationed myself behind the goals so that I could have a word with Ron and watch him in action at close quarters. It happened that he had a nightmare. He saved some tremendous shots from close range, but he let in several optimistic long-range pots at goal as Barnsley got seven. Whenever he had to pick the ball out of the net, he saw my grinning face. 'I bet you've got backache,' I suggested when we met afterwards. 'Yes,' he acknowledged. 'And now I suppose I'm going to get earache listening to you gloat.'

Ron, incidentally, was a very brave player of fast bowling as an opener. Andy Roberts, who said very little but must rank among the most hostile pacemen of all time, told me that when opening the attack for Hampshire he had given Ron a real pasting on a helpful wicket. 'Dickie, he must have been black and blue,' he said. 'But he wouldn't quit.' He didn't at Barnsley either, and one of his best saves came right at the end with the match hopelessly lost.

Much more recently, I turned up to watch Sheffield Wednesday battle it out with Everton in a long-running FA Cup saga. Wednesday's tremendous effort eventually petered out as they went down 5–0 at home, a strange result in view of the close nature of the three previous draws. Deep into the second half, a home fan spotted me in the stand and shouted up: 'Hey, Dickie, can't you get them off for bad light and give us another chance?'

In the old days, before all the nation had radios and televisions, the local paper used to bring the news of Barnsley's exploits in away games. Cup replays had to be staged in the afternoons, because there were no floodlights and it was never easy to get time off work to attend. A keen fan, faced with the certainty of missing a replay involving Barnsley, worked out an ingenious scheme to hear the result almost as soon as it was available. The chap happened to be a pigeon fancier, so he handed his best bird to a pal who, being on shifts in the pit, was in the envied position of seeing the tie live. 'As soon as the whistle blows, you send the bird with the score and it'll reach our house just about the same time as I get home

AND THE GOAL WAS SCORED BY...

The chap happened to be a pigeon fancier ...

from t' factory,' he instructed.

The plan worked well. The bird was taken to the ground in a basket and the miner got a good position from which he could release it right on the bell. It was a very close match with Barnsley getting the vital goal very near the end. Leaping and cheering with the rest of the home supporters, the miner suddenly remembered his responsibility. Pulling the bird roughly out of the basket, he shouted into its startled little face: 'Barnsley's won 1–0,' and threw it high into the air.

Soccer transfer fees have 'gone through the roof' in my lifetime, with money apparently no object to some of the bigger clubs. Somehow, though, I don't think Barnsley will ever pay the world record price for any player and they are the club who get my regular support.

One of the big spenders in his time has been Brian Clough, the outspoken manager of Nottingham Forest. I can well imagine there is a lot of truth in a little tale about Cloughie. He was having a discussion with another Football League manager, who enjoyed boasting about his success in the transfer market. 'I paid only £25,000 for so and so,' he said, 'He's doing so well that 100,000 wouldn't buy him.' 'I agree there,' quipped Brian, 'and I'm one of them.'

I have been told cricket and golf do not mix and that the one can affect the other. This may be true in some cases, but there are some notable exceptions. Brian Close, as we have noted earlier, got down to single figures both left and right handed, which has to be something of a record at any level, and I guess he could be the world champion in any competition where the players had to switch round after each hole. Ray Illingworth is a difficult man to beat, too, and there have been many other good golfers among the cricket fraternity.

Golf is a tremendous social game and was very popular on the circuit in the days before the Sunday League, when cricketers always had one day off each week on a regular basis. It could, therefore, have been four of them who played at this particular club one weekend. The first tee happened to be a short walk from the club house, so it was customary for the players to bang a bell-like contraption once they had driven off, thus saving the inconvenience of too many people gathering in the teeing area.

It was a very busy day and a lengthy queue developed around the club house. The four duly took their turn but, after they had departed, ten minutes went by without the expected sound of the bell. Fifteen minutes elapsed and eventually the next group set off, assuming that the others had forgotten to do the needful. When they got to the tee, however, they discovered one man laid on the floor with the other three fighting furiously. Eventually they managed to separate them and asked what had provoked the dispute. 'Well,' explained one, clearly having had the worst of the exchanges, 'my partner had a stroke on the tee and these two wanted to count it.'

Now it is a bit surprising that Rugby League has never 'taken off' in South Yorkshire. Comparatively recently a professional team has operated in Sheffield, but that is about it. In contrast, only a few miles away in the mining areas of West Yorkshire, the game has a great tradition. The mining areas around Featherstone, Wakefield and Castleford have produced some brilliant Rugby footballers. I haven't really come into much contact with Rugby League, although I sometimes meet some of the top names at various functions, but I know that there are some hard physical exchanges.

The professional clubs recruit from the Rugby Union world and I did hear of the keen young forward who switched codes. He was a very big, powerful lad, but he had not been on the field long on his League debut when one of the opposition punched him on the nose in a tackle. As the pair regained their feet, they stood eyeball to eyeball and everyone waited for the exchange of blows that seemed certain to come. Instead the youngster, his nose streaming blood, held out his hand. 'Why on earth did you do that?' asked one of his team-mates. 'You ought to have cracked him one.' 'Oh, I did better than that,' explained the new boy. 'I made him feel a cad.'

Perhaps he did, but I feel the prevailing attitude is more accurately summed up by the prop forward who said: 'From my first game I realised that it was best to get the retaliation in first.' It isn't only the forwards who can be hard men. One club chairman, driving through the town late on a Saturday night, passed a fight on a street corner. 'Wasn't that Smith, our winger, in the middle of all that?' asked his wife, who took an interest in these things. 'Yes,' he agreed. 'Typical of our team – there were three of our forwards stood back watching him.' It was, incidentally, Alex Murphy, the multi-talented Rugby League player and coach, who said: 'Never trust a forward with his own teeth.'

I do not have much connection with boxing either, but I like the story about the fighter of average ability who found himself out of his depth against a much more skilled opponent. He realised he was in trouble in the first round as he took a fair amount of punishment to the head and the body. 'We're doing all right,' his second assured him when he got back to his corner. 'We're letting him use up his energy with punches which aren't hurting us a bit.'

The second round followed the same pattern. The traffic was mostly one way and the boxer collapsed onto his stool at the interval, his face a mass of cuts and bruises. 'That's great,' enthused his second. 'We have him in a lot of trouble now. He's really getting tired hitting us with all those punches and we aren't hurt. When he runs out of steam our turn will come and we'll take control.'

Unfortunately the third round proved even more one-sided and our hero was covered in blood when the bell went. Slumping down, he turned to his second and, through swollen lips, mumbled: 'Before you say anything, we're retiring. I think he's broken our bloody nose.'

And so to the gentler sport of snooker. Once regarded as a back-street activity, it has been elevated into a major television attraction by the skills and good manners of Steve Davis, Joe Johnson, Dennis Taylor and their colleagues on the green baize. Snooker players seem such perfect sportsmen and are always immaculately turned out. It is, however, a game that lends itself to cheating in the guise of 'hustling'.

All over the country, clubs have their top players and in one of these the star in question was enjoying a good night playing for £10 a time. The group of challengers gradually thinned out as one by one the hopefuls 'bit the dust' until he had no-one left to play. 'Are you all chicken?' he enquired. A stranger who had been standing at the bar watching the play quietly indicated that he was prepared to take his chance. 'I'll have to borrow a cue,' he said as he took off his jacket and carefully folded it over a chair.

'Well, it's a waste of time, but there's nobody else to play,' said the champion. 'Does anyone want a side bet on him to make it more interesting?' Not surprisingly the invitation provoked little response, although an old man in the corner suddenly spoke up. 'I'll have £10 on the stranger,' he said. This caused a ripple of amusement, but the laughter did not last long because the champion was overwhelmed in no time. The visitor won the first frame with a break of 55, the second with a run of 60 and the third by dint of some skilful snookers.

Finally the locals had to admit defeat. 'Tell me, what made you back me?' the stranger asked his one supporter. 'You didn't know I was much too good for loudmouth over there, and I had to play with any old cue.' 'I noticed you had your own chalk in your jacket pocket,' came the reply, 'It's been my experience that only someone who is

more than useful and in regular practice carries chalk
about with him.'

||| 10 |||

It Makes You Laugh

Yorkshiremen, they say, have an odd sense of humour, but, as with everything else, we'll keep it and let the rest of the world get about their own business. It also takes a lot to impress us. When Fred Trueman first went to Australia, he was given a guided tour of Sydney by a local with a lot of native pride. Everywhere they went, Fred's guide boasted about how big and splendid things were Down Under and how small and insignificant things were in England by comparison. All over the place they went, seeing the tallest, longest, heaviest, widest, most admired sights in the world. Fred stood it for as long as he could, not wishing to upset his host, but in the end he could not resist just one comment to balance the books. 'What's that then?' he enquired, pointing at the Sydney Harbour bridge. Immediately he received a long lecture on the marvels of its structure. Making the most of a slight pause in the narrative, Fred suddenly said: 'I'll tell thee summat. It's built out of steel from Sheffield and you buggers haven't paid for it all yet.'

Village cricket is very important in Yorkshire and there can surely be nowhere else in the world where so many cricket fields exist in so small an area. Sometimes they are little more than cow pastures, rescued for four short months to provide the playing area for the local youngsters – and the not so young, for that matter. In one village, the secretary of the team made an annual trip up to the squire's house to seek the use of a field for the summer. It was a polite ritual and, as expected, he was given permission. As he was leaving, however, the squire asked if he would do him a favour. 'I've an old dog that needs putting down. I know you have a gun, so I'd be obliged if you would do the job for me. I haven't the heart to shoot him myself after all these years.'

Off the secretary marched to get his gun, taking the dog with him. Then he went into some woods on the edge of the village, shot the unfortunate animal and was burying it when another member of the cricket club happened to pass by. 'What are you doing there, then?' came the query. The secretary decided to have a bit of a joke. 'You wouldn't believe it,' he said. 'But old Squire Bosomworth has said we can't have the cricket field this year, so I've shot his dog and I'm digging a grave.' Seeing the evidence before his own eyes, the team member cycled away, muttering ominously under his breath about the ruling classes.

The secretary thought nothing more about it until a week later when the two met by chance in the village pub. His naive friend came up and, whispering out of the corner of his mouth, imparted some worrying news. 'Don't worry about the field. I thought about what you told me and I don't think you were going far enough to make the squire change his mind. I shot two of his cows last night and if the greedy old bugger doesn't offer the field this week, I'll put two more down next time.'

It may well have been the same secretary who received an anxious letter from touring opponents whom they entertained once a season. The visitors had been very worried about the state of the pitch on their last visit and were keen to get some assurance about improvements before committing themselves. The secretary, anxious to retain the fixture which was popular with all his players, wrote back stating that 'without any doubt our strip will be like a billiard table'. Came the big day and nothing had altered. The ball leapt as it had always done from a variety of holes and bumps, causing a number of painful injuries. 'I see what you mean about a billiard table,' acknowledged the visitors' captain. 'It's definitely green and got at least six pockets.'

Tours are, of course, very popular with cricketers and some clubs do not even have a ground. They are usually called Nomads or Wanderers and they save the trouble and expense of maintaining their own facilities by playing all their games away. The secretary of such an organisation set out on one trip with £2,000 cash in his pocket to cover hotel and travelling expenses. Together with his party he journeyed south and settled into a neat country hotel which was to serve as headquarters for the week's chosen activities.

As is the nature of things, the first night turned into something of a drinking session and the hardier spirits, including the secretary, moved on to a night club in a neighbouring town. They got back to base in the small hours, full of alcohol and high hopes. Came the dawn and retribution. The secretary came back to the land of the living with his head throbbing, roused by the sound of the more sober of his colleagues knocking on his door. 'Come in,' he croaked. 'How are you this morning?' the star batsman asked. Regaining his scattered senses, the secretary fumbled under his pillow. With a moan he fell back on the bed. 'To tell the truth,' he moaned, 'I don't feel two grand.'

Local club cricket also allows players to continue long after they have passed the normal age of retirement at first-class level. Many, many veterans can be seen in action still enjoying themselves in their fifties, sixties and even seventies. When an old stalwart medium-paced bowler died, the vicar made due reference to his prowess in a long oration. 'Let us think of George, in his prime,' he advised. 'Let us think, too, of George now in a cricketer's heaven. Let us hope that he will spend eternity wheeling away on endless sunny days and on a perfect pitch, bowling and bowling.' 'Good grief,' observed one of the village ancients, 'The thought of that would have killed old George.'

Talking about funerals, I liked a weekly newspaper report I once saw on one for an old Dales shepherd. It read: 'Dales people came from many miles to pay their last respects to Mr Sowden, who was well known and very popular. All concerned enjoyed the fine sermon from the Rev. Peabody, who dwelt at length on the life and times of a shepherd. Unfortunately, a cloud was cast over enjoyment of the proceedings when Mr Sowden's old dog Bess collapsed and died.'

There are some close-knit communities in Yorkshire and the inhabitants tend to regard the village boundary as the edge of civilisation. A newcomer took over the restaurant on the outskirts of a country town and had not been living there long when he turned up at the local garage. According to custom, the owner, who did all the jobs himself, came out to serve the petrol, which was somewhat dearer than in the larger areas of population. 'You ought to get these pumps on the self-service basis,' said the restaurateur. 'It's silly that I should have to pay you to do a job I could do myself. If I served myself you could reduce the price of your petrol.'

Next night, the garage man and his wife turned up at the restaurant. After studying the menu, the garage man ordered two omelettes, adding: 'Just bring the eggs. There's no point in paying the chef to do a job the wife could do just as well.'

It could be argued that the situation reflected a lack of communication, and there are two other examples which come to mind. The first involved Alan Knott, the Kent wicketkeeper. Bradford Park Avenue's ancient pavilion has since been demolished, but when Knotty played there with Kent, a little tea bar nestled underneath at the back of the structure, staffed by a series of redoubtable ladies.

Feeling a bit peckish in the middle of the afternoon, Alan strolled round to the tea bar. 'Got any nats, love?' he enquired. His accent clearly confused the situation. 'Pardon?' 'Got any nats?' he persisted, indicating in mime the act of opening a packet of nuts and taking one out. At last the light shone through.

'Oh, yes,' said the female in charge, looking around under the counter before straightening up. 'But we've only cheese and onion until I get to the supermarket.'

The second also centres on an outsider opening a new store in a Yorkshire village. One of his first customers happened to be a local farmer, who spent some time struggling unsuccessfully to find what he sought in the rows of neatly stacked shelves. 'Can I be of any assistance, sir?' asked the owner. 'Aye, lad, 'as ta getten any leeters?' At this the owner brightened because including a wide range of wines had been a special idea of his. 'We certainly have, sir, were you thinking of litres of red or white?' 'Nah, faure leeters to get a bit on a blaze going,' came the earthy reply.

||| 11 |||

Bits and Pieces

There is an expression common, I imagine, throughout the country to the effect that 'you have to laugh, otherwise you would cry'. Equally, people have widely differing senses of humour, so that what is hilariously funny to one might not even raise a smile on another face. In the circumstances, putting together a collection of 'funnies' involves taking something of a risk. Well, we've got this far, so to finish I have recorded a few of the stories from outside the sporting scene that have at least made me chuckle.

Two parents were talking about their children and discussing what the future might hold. 'What's your John going to be when he leaves school?' asked one. 'I don't know,' replied the other. 'He is so uncertain about everything. First it's one thing and then another. He just can't make up his mind and when he does get an idea into his head for any length of time, it is usually nonsense.' 'He's ready made for one career then,' came the confident assertion. 'He'll make an ideal weather forecaster.'

A group of people, having been invited out to dinner, were gathered in the drawing room after the meal admiring a fine collection of animal heads suitably mounted and arranged around the walls. Lions, tigers, antelopes, zebra – nearly every species was represented in a dazzling array of trophies. 'Good gracious,' said one of the guests. 'There must be many a story behind some of these.' He indicated the heads with a broad sweep of his arm. 'You must have taken some terrible risks to shoot some of them.' 'Not really,' said the host modestly. 'The tricky bit was getting them out of the zoo in the dark.'

A Barnsley woman – and there is no more thrifty person anywhere – took her small son into town to buy him a raincoat. They duly tried on a number of garments in the shop before finding one that was the right size and colour. The woman buttoned it up and ordered the boy to go outside and stand in the rain. After a few minutes, the shop assistant made an anxious enquiry as to what she was doing. 'I had to wait for a wet day,' the woman explained. 'After all, you don't think I'm going to pay good money for a coat unless I am certain it is waterproof. I'll call him in in a few minutes and if he's dry underneath we'll take it.'

A man went into a florist's shop and bought a bouquet of flowers. 'They are for my wife, so there is no need to include a card. She will know who sent them,' he told the assistant. Later in the morning the florist received a panic-stricken telephone call from the lady. 'You have just delivered some flowers, I would like to know who sent them,' she asked. 'I am sorry, madam, we are not at liberty to divulge that information,' she was told. Literally within minutes, the lady arrived at the shop with the flowers. 'Look here, you had better take them back,' she said. 'If my husband discovers my admirer is sending me flowers he'll kill me.'

A middle-aged couple were invited to a party at which the husband spent the whole evening talking to a series of pretty young girls. As they drove home his wife observed: 'I am really impressed with your performance tonight.' 'You mean the fact that I can still hold the attention of attractive young women,' he suggested. 'No,' she said, 'I mean the fact that you can hold your stomach in for so long and still manage to breathe.'

It might have been as a result of that very party that

the wife in question was asked about the husband's roving eye. A well-meaning lady friend raised the subject in casual conversation, as well-meaning ladies have a habit of doing. 'I noticed your husband spending all evening talking to those young girls,' she said in a sympathetic tone. 'Don't you worry about him getting a reputation as a lady killer?' 'Oh, I never worry,' came the reply. 'He's already well known for that.' 'What, being a lady killer?' 'Yes, he usually bores them to death.'

A business man attending a big function discovered when he arrived that all the guests ahead of him in the queue to be announced had titles after their name. Being plain John Smith but not wanting to appear inferior, he had to think quickly. When it came to his turn, the footman boomed: 'Mr John Smith CPE and his lady wife.' 'I didn't know you had letters after your name,' she said as they began to mingle. 'I don't,' he replied. 'Then what does CPE stand for?' she persisted. 'Can't pass exams,' he said with a smile.

A young commercial traveller – they tend to call them company representatives these days – found himself struggling to get suitable accommodation in a strange town. Not having been in the job long, he had no established list of acceptable establishments at reasonable prices, so he had to stay at a rather superior hotel which turned out to be a good deal more expensive than he had expected.

Still, he reasoned, it was only for one night. To economise, he decided to forego dinner, so by the time he went down for breakfast his stomach felt his throat had been cut. Predictably, he was first into the dining room at 7.30 as soon as it opened. Working out that he could also save on lunch if he ate a large meal, he swooped on the help-yourself section of starters, filling a dish with grapefruit and cereal and snatching a large piece of bread. The bread, however, proved to be rock hard. This gave him an idea. If he complained loudly enough he might get something off the bill, he reasoned. 'Fetch me the manager,' he shouted. 'I have stayed in top hotels all over the world and this is the worst breakfast I have come across. This bread is terrible. How dare you serve it?' He repeated the tirade when the manager arrived, but that gentleman waited until he drew breath and then said: 'Well, if you have stayed in so many hotels you should recognise the display bread. It's been specially treated and varnished.'

Now we come to after-dinner speaking. This is a hazardous business for both the speaker and his audience. Sometimes there is an instant rapport, while on other occasions the whole affair can become an embarrassment. As I see it, there are two types of speaker. There are those who rely entirely on humour and those who have something important to say. Often the latter are famous in their own field, so they command instant attention.

The trouble is that the two can become mixed to an unfortunate extent. Learie Constantine, the brilliant West Indian all-rounder who later became a leading figure outside sport, was once invited to speak at a cricket league dinner in Yorkshire. By some mischance he had been placed last on the toast list and at least two of those taking their turn before him went on far too long.

Obviously a lot of those present wanted to hear Constantine, but by the time he got to his feet it was very late and many were quietly making their way to the exits. 'I don't know why you asked me to come,' he said. 'Tonight has been a waste of everyone's time.' A harsh judgment maybe, but he was probably right, and I think that too many speakers can spoil a cricket dinner at which a lot of those attending also want to have a word with their friends.

It is not easy to get a speaker to sit down once he is into his stride and some simply cannot tell when they have 'outworn their welcome'. In one instance, a long-winded local dignitary had been holding forth for so long that

After-dinner speaking can be a hazardous business for both the speaker and his audience.

most of his audience had switched off. One guest, having had too much to drink, finally lost patience and hurled an empty wine bottle in an attempt to stem the flow of words that had been coming from the top table.

Unfortunately the alcohol affected his aim, so the bottle hit a man slightly to the left of the intended target. The victim slumped forward, his head resting on the table. Immediately there was a rush to render first aid, but the would-be helpers were checked by a weak voice which implored: 'Hit me again, I can still hear him.'

Journalists have to sit through more speeches than the average member of society because it is part of their job, and they are obliged to take notes, too, so they cannot just drift off and let it all pass over their heads. One experienced representative of the Press attended a particularly boring dinner at which the chief guest took the opportunity to hammer home a lot of obscure points to the captive assembly. On and on he droned.

As the speaker at last paused for breath and shuffled through a formidable sheaf of notes, the man seated next to the journalist murmured: 'I'd give a fiver to shut him up.' 'Really?' said the newspaper man, who wrote briefly on a strip torn from his menu and passed it along the table. 'You'd better get ready to pay up, then,' he continued, 'the old windbag will sit down within the next couple of minutes.' Sure enough, on receiving the note, which had been handed along, the speaker muttered a few more polite comments and hurriedly regained his seat to thankful rather than enthusiastic applause. 'That's marvellous,' said the man, handing over a fiver. 'But how did you do it?' 'Easy,' admitted the journalist. 'The note said "Your flies are undone."'

The wine usually flows at dinners and I like the little aside about the small boy who watched his father putting on his dress suit before asking: 'Why do you keep wearing that daddy? You know it always gives you a headache.'

Three Yorkshiremen, strangers, although they lived in the same town, happened to find themselves adrift in a boat on the high seas. Their ship had sunk for some reason or another and it did not look as if they were going to survive the experience. A couple of days went by with no sign of rescue and, as they grew weaker, they began to confide in each other.

'I'm afraid I have been terribly unfaithful to my wife,' admitted one. 'I have never been able to resist a pretty face and in my time as a traveller I had some moments. They're all over now, I suppose, and the good thing is that my little Mary will never know. She wouldn't have understood, so it's a consolation really that her faith in me will remain intact.'

'I know how you feel,' agreed the second. 'It's the drink with me. I've been telling my wife all these years that my wage was much smaller than it really was so that I could go out with the boys on the way home from the office to have a few pints. Always told her I was working late and she never found out. Now she never will.'

'Haven't you any little vices?' they asked their companion, who had been listening with rapt attention. 'Well,' he said, 'I've some good news and some bad. The good news is that I can see a ship on the horizon and it's making its way in our direction. The bad news is that I'm a terrible gossip.'

It may have been the same Yorkshiremen – or three others from the same part of the country – who were standing at the bar in their local one night. The conversation drifted along the usual lines, taking in the weather, what had been on television and sport, but gradually two of them realised that their companion, normally free with his opinions, had not said much more than the occasional word all evening.

'Now then, Ted lad, you've been very quiet. Haven't you got anything to say tonight? Is something wrong,' they enquired. Ted gazed sadly into his pint and nodded his head. 'I'm afraid there is,' he admitted. 'My wife has packed her bags, taken the car and run off with the insurance man,' he said. There was a long silence. His friends shuffled their feet and gazed into space, not knowing quite what to say. 'That's very bad luck,' one eventually ventured. 'You must be very sorry about that.' 'I am,' confirmed Ted. 'I'd paid £75 for a service only yesterday.'

||| 12 |||

... and Finally

When you are chatting with friends, the time flies by, with one topic leading to another. Writing this book has been much the same for me. I feel I am talking to good friends, and I know from the number of people who come up for a word at various games that I have plenty. This is something for which I am very grateful.

Obviously I know some a lot better than others and I am proud to say that among my close friends are Lord and Lady Mason. Roy Mason was, of course, the Member of Parliament for Barnsley and some time ago he took me on a conducted tour of the House of Commons.

Well, in the 1988 season I stood in my hundredth international, which happened to be the Texaco Trophy clash between England and the West Indies at Lord's. Before that game Lord Mason telephoned me to say that he wanted to celebrate the occasion by giving me dinner in the House of Lords after the game.

That rounded the day off in magnificent style for me, and after a quick shower I got all dressed up and rushed out of the ground, running down the long drive to the Grace Gates to hail a taxi. There is often a lot of competition for cabs, but I was lucky to get one more or less straight away. Jumping in a bit out of breath, I gasped: 'Lord's, as quick as you can.' The driver looked round puzzled. 'Blimey, Dickie,' he shouted, 'you're there already. You can't want a lift up to the pavilion.' I laughed. 'The House of Lords, my man,' I replied, pretending to put on a bit of style. 'Oh, I see,' said the driver. 'They need a good umpire down there now for all those political debates I suppose.'

Actually, we had a bit of a problem during the Texaco game. My colleague was Nigel Plews, a former fraud squad detective, who is officially listed at 6 ft. 6½ in. There are no hard and fast rules about which end the umpires stand at, so we usually just decide between ourselves before we get out into the middle. In championship matches we change over after both sides have had their first innings, of course, but in limited-overs games we remain at the same ends throughout.

At Lord's we settled for me going to the Nursery End, which meant Nigel had his back to the pavilion. Apparently this created a lot of difficulties for the television cameramen, who had trouble in getting a good picture of the action because Nigel was simply too tall. They asked if we could change over, but this was clearly impossible. You can't mess about with the traditions of the game. In the end they had to find some blocks of wood to raise the cameras and after that they were able to manage all right.

One of the ways in which I meet a lot of people is through speaking at dinners. I get literally hundreds of requests and sometimes I think I ought to have either a social secretary or a business manager, particularly on the days when the telephone never stops ringing. Apart from the official part of these functions, I appreciate the opportunity of chatting 'off the record' with cricket enthusiasts, who always have a lot of questions, and I really believe that these functions are important in communicating between the various levels of the game.

Other sports have a significant social side, but I doubt if any of them can compete with cricket. Apart from the dinners, there are all the societies – Wombwell Cricket Lovers, just down the road from me, is one of the most famous in the world – and many of the top personalities spend hundreds of hours in the winter 'spreading the gospel'.

One snag can involve finding the venue. One chap I know very well – to save his blushes I'll not give his name – travelled a long way one bleak winter night to the Huddersfield area and arrived in good time at the appointed place. There was no sign of activity in the car park, but he sat in his vehicle waiting for someone to turn up.

It was very cold and he began to feel a bit put out. Eventually another car arrived. Two men got out and hurried into the club. 'At last,' he thought, briskly following them. 'It's about time you came,' he snapped as he marched into the room, 'and I would have thought you could have done something to make sure a few people turned up.' He was met with a puzzled frown. 'Oh, you're our speaker for this month,' said one of the two locals as the penny dropped, 'but you aren't due until tomorrow night. We've just come to put the chairs out.'

I always double check the dates, but I did have one spot of bother, also in Huddersfield. I thought I knew the town very well and I have been to many of the cricket grounds in the area, but this time I could not find the meeting place. I drove around for about an hour in the dark, ending up down little country lanes and getting more and more confused.

Although I always allow at least twice the necessary travelling time, just to be on the safe side, I began to get a bit desperate. Finally I drove back into the centre of town and went to the police station to explain my predicament. 'I should have thought you would have known your way around here,' said the officer on duty. He then gave me directions. They sounded very complicated. 'Look, mate,' I said, 'I'm going to be late if I'm not careful and I think I lost you at the third left turn.' The upshot was that a patrol car which happened to be going in the right direction led the way for me. When we got a bit off the beaten track, he put his flashing light on so I did not lose him and I discovered I was the first speaker at that particular organisation to have a police escort.

When I have any real distance to travel, I usually ask for an overnight stay. I spoke at a dinner for a good friend of mine, Ted Markwick, who is in the car phone business. This was near Trowbridge in Wiltshire, and he would not hear of my staying in a hotel. He and his wife, Chris, insisted that I spent the night at their home. 'I think we can find room for you,' he said. 'Look, I don't want to be a nuisance,' I told him, but I need not have worried. He has a wonderful home and I thought I was arriving at Windsor Castle when I drove through the gates. That was one function I really did enjoy.

Another pal who has looked after me very well down the years is my chemist, Bryan Ellison, and before I undertake any trip overseas I hurry along to his shop in Huddersfield Road, Barnsley.

He provides me with all the pills and potions I need to keep going. Chemists, of course, have the reputation of being able to read the worst handwriting because, I suppose, they have to understand all those squiggles on prescriptions. One well-known after-dinner speaker received a letter from a cricket league secretary obviously inviting him to attend a particular gathering. The trouble was he could not make out a word of it. Having given the matter some thought, he decided to ask the local chemist. He duly went into the shop, put the letter on the counter and asked: 'What do you make of that?' The chemist looked at it and said: 'Just wait a minute.' He disappeared into the back of the premises and returned shortly with a large bottle and a plastic spoon. Handing them over, together with the letter, he said: 'Take a spoonful three times a day and if you aren't any better in a week, go back to the doctor.'

We are a fairly close-knit community on the cricket circuit, with players, officials, umpires and the Press mixing in a generally friendly way. We are like ships in the night, but year after year we bump into each other up and down the country and have the odd chat and a drink or a meal together.

I am convinced that this creates a healthy atmosphere. There are, of course, disagreements, but overall it is good for, say, journalists to be able to come and check on incidents to make sure they get the facts right. Through this sort of contact, more permanent friendships grow and, as I have mentioned earlier, I am grateful for the help that John Callaghan, of the *Yorkshire Evening Post*, has given me in putting together this book.

He spends his summer covering the affairs of Yorkshire, who, incidentally, have a big following of newspaper men all providing a service for a public who take a keen interest in the team's progress. This involves spending the same late hours as the players on the motorways, dashing from one game to the next, and there is always the danger of getting lost.

Some seasons ago, some of the Yorkshire Press party were approaching Bournemouth in the early hours of the morning after a long drive and one of them decided he knew a short cut. This is often the case – an individual remembering vaguely the route he took two or three seasons previously. In this case, the short cut turned into something of a disaster, for having passed a sign indicating eight miles to Bournemouth at about one o'clock, they were still weaving about the minor roads an hour later. In the end, they were lucky to flag down a taxi driver who led them back to civilisation.

In another season, Yorkshire stayed in Bristol, but used a different hotel some way away from the cricket ground. As the players arrived for breakfast on the morning of the game there was a lot of discussion about the best way to take. John's travelling companion dismissed all suggestions. 'We'll lead the way,' he said. 'I've stayed here before and I know the quickest route.'

So off they went in convoy, with John at the front. He received a lot of instructions in the early stages, but became increasingly worried by the lengthy silence that developed as the miles went by. His 'navigator' was anxiously peering out of the windows and appeared totally lost. Suddenly he brightened up. 'It's all right now, I recognise this bit of road,' he said cheerfully. 'So do I,' John replied, 'we're back at the hotel!' There were a lot of flashing lights and hooting horns behind, but fortunately the rain was pouring down, so although the team arrived at the right place a bit late it did not matter.

And so to one last cricket story. In one of my very first games for Yorkshire I found myself partnering a senior batsman who had better remain nameless. I have to admit that I had a bit of a rough time. I played and missed and got one or two edges that just beat the clutching hands of the slips. Things were not all that much better at the other end. In fact, they were worse, and the pair of us survived more by good luck than management for quite a while.

Eventually, however, I gained a bit of confidence and picked up one or two singles. Still the struggle continued at the other end. Then, I hit two lovely fours through the covers and I felt very good. Down the pitch came my well-known team-mate. I went to meet him expecting some words of praise. 'I can't work it out,' he said, looking me up and down as though I were improperly dressed. 'How come they're bowling so well at me and giving you all that rubbish to hit?' It's a funny game, cricket. Happy playing, watching . . . and umpiring.